The Newbery Medal

The Newbery Medal, the first award of its kind, is the official recognition by the American Library Association of the most distinguished children's book published during the previous year. It is the primary and best known award in the field of children's literature.

Frederic G. Melcher first proposed the award, to be named after the eighteenth-century English bookseller John Newbery, to the Children's Librarian Section of the American Library Association meeting on June 21, 1921. His proposal was met with enthusiastic acceptance and was officially adopted by the ALA Executive Board in 1922. The award itself was commissioned by Mr. Melcher to be created by the artist Rene Paul Chambellan.

Mr. Melcher's formal agreement with the ALA Board included the following statement of purpose: "To encourage original creative work in the field of books for children. To emphasize to the public that contributions to the literature for children deserve similar recognition to poetry, plays, or novels. To give those librarians, who make it their life work to serve children's reading interests, an opportunity to encourage good writing in this field."

The medal is awarded by the Association for Library Service to Children, a division of the ALA. Other books on the final ballot for the Newbery are considered Newbery Honor Books.

In evaluating the candidates for exceptional children's literature, the committee members must consider the following criteria:

- The interpretation of the theme or concept
- Presentation of the information, including accuracy, clarity, and organization
- Development of plot
- Delineation of characters
- Delineation of setting
- Appropriateness of style
- Excellence of presentation for a child audience
- The book as a contribution to literature as a whole. The committee is to base its decision primarily on the text of the book, although other aspects of a book, such as illustrations or overall design, may be considered if they are an integral part of the story being conveyed.

Titles in

Adoniram
and Other Selections by Newbery Authors

Christmas on the Prairie
and Other Selections by Newbery Authors

Dancing Tom
and Other Selections by Newbery Authors

For a Horse
and Other Selections by Newbery Authors

For the Sake of Freedom
and Other Selections by Newbery Authors

The Highest Hit
and Other Selections by Newbery Authors

The Horse of the War God
and Other Selections by Newbery Authors

A Knife for Tomaso
and Other Selections by Newbery Authors

Lighthouse Island
and Other Selections by Newbery Authors

Little Sioux Girl
and Other Selections by Newbery Authors

Lone Cowboy
and Other Selections by Newbery Authors

The Wise Soldier of Sellebak
and Other Selections by Newbery Authors

Christmas on the Prairie

and Other Selections by Newbery Authors

Edited by Martin H. Greenberg
and Charles G. Waugh

Gareth Stevens Publishing
A WORLD ALMANAC EDUCATION GROUP COMPANY

The American Library Association receives a portion of the sale price of each volume in *The Newbery Authors Collection.*

The Newbery Medal was named for eighteenth-century British bookseller John Newbery. It is awarded annually by the Association for Library Service to Children, a division of the American Library Association, to the author of the most distinguished contribution to American literature for children. The American Library Association has granted the use of the Newbery name.

A note from the editors: These stories reflect many of the values, opinions, and standards of language that existed during the times in which the works were written. Much of the language is also a reflection of the personalities and lifestyles of the stories' narrators and characters. Readers today may strongly disagree, for example, with the ways in which members of various groups, such as women or ethnic minorities, are described. In compiling these works, however, we felt that it was important to capture as much of the flavor and character of the original stories as we could. Rather than delete or alter language that is intrinsically important to the literature, we hope that these stories will give parents, educators, and young readers a chance to think and talk about the many ways in which people lead their lives, view the world, and express their feelings about what they have lived through.

Please visit our web site at: www.garethstevens.com
For a free color catalog describing Gareth Stevens Publishing's list of high-quality books and multimedia programs, call 1-800-542-2595 (USA) or 1-800-461-9120 (Canada). Gareth Stevens Publishing's Fax: (414) 332-3567.

Library of Congress Cataloging-in-Publication Data

Christmas on the prairie and other selections by Newbery authors / edited by Martin H. Greenberg and Charles G. Waugh.
p. cm. — (The Newbery authors collection)
Contents: Christmas on the prairie/Lois Lenski — Kapugen/Jean Craighead George — Hungry old witch/Charles J. Finger — Feed mill/Walter D. Edmonds — Wonderful mirror/Charles J. Finger — Aunt Charity arrives in New England/Lois Lenski.
ISBN 0-8368-2950-6 (lib. bdg.)
1. Children's stories, American. [1. Christmas—Fiction. 2. Short stories.] I. Greenberg, Martin Harry. II. Waugh, Charles. III. Series.
PZ5.C4738 2001
[Fic]—dc21 2001031105

First published in 2001 by
Gareth Stevens Publishing
A World Almanac Education Group Company
330 West Olive Street, Suite 100
Milwaukee, WI 53212 USA

Cover illustration: Joel Bucaro

Printed in the United States of America

1 2 3 4 5 6 7 8 9 05 04 03 02 01

Contents

Edited by Martin H. Greenberg and Charles G. Waugh

Christmas on the Prairie
by Lois Lenski 7

Kapugen
by Jean Craighead George 42

The Hungry Old Witch
by Charles J. Finger 64

The Feed Mill
by Walter D. Edmonds 75

The Wonderful Mirror
by Charles J. Finger 94

Aunt Charity Arrives in New England
by Lois Lenski 107

Author Biographies 148

Newbery Award-Winning Books 151

Christmas on the Prairie

Lois Lenski

"Only nine more sleeps till Christmas!" exclaimed Delores.

"Oh, I just can't wait to see what I'm gonna get," said Fernetta. The two girls put their heads together, giggling.

"Jacob drew my name," whispered Delores. "Tell me what he's got for me."

"No, sir, it's a secret," said Fernetta. "But it's something nice."

"Please, Fernetta, please." Delores jumped up and down. "Tell me."

But Fernetta wouldn't. "I bet that old Emil Holzhauer will give me a fly-swatter or something crazy. He's loco!"

The girls burst into peals of laughter.

"Boy! Won't he look purty dressed up in whiskers?"

Emil's head came round the curtain. "Boo!" he shouted. "I'm gonna be Santa Claus and scare the little kids." He held his mask up in front of his face, and the girls tried to snatch it off.

The Oak Leaf children were getting ready for their

Christmas program, and had already drawn names for the exchange of gifts. The first snow had long been forgotten. Other snows had come in late November and early December. The prairie was white now, surrounded by snow-topped buttes. Snow was an everyday experience, while overshoes and heavy wraps had become daily necessities.

The program was to be held in the evening, to make it easier for the parents to come. The children worked hard to get ready. They made a big fireplace out of cardboard cartons, and pasted red lined crepe paper on to look like bricks. Darrell made a base for the Christmas tree, bought by Emil long ago in November and kept carefully hidden in the barn until now. Chris Bieber and his wife, Vera Mae, who had no children, brought a battery and a string of lights for the tree. The boys helped string the lights on while the girls stood and admired.

The desks were turned around to face the back of the room. Jacob and Wilmer Sticklemeyer stretched the curtain wire across, and hung the stage curtains on it. This made it possible to use the teacher-age kitchen for a dressing room. The Biebers and the Hummels brought lanterns, one for kerosene and the other a gas lantern with a mantle, which made a very bright light.

Evening came all too soon. The people arrived early, as soon as evening chores were done. There were the Hummels, Sniders, Engleharts and the Sticklemeyers, who had children in school, and the Burgards, Hunstads and Becklers, whose children were grown up now. All the families brought their younger children, who were soon running around the schoolroom. The last ones to arrive were Johannes and Minna Wagner.

"So much to do," complained Mrs. Wagner. "My work, it never gets done." The other mothers nodded their heads in agreement.

"Is it going to snow?" asked Mrs. Englehart. "Ain't it about time for a real good storm?"

"Ach no! We want no storms this winter," said Mrs. Pete Hummel. "I remember a storm once . . ." The talk went on and on.

At eight o'clock, Miss Martin herded the children into her bedroom to put on their costumes.

"I brought my records," said Ruby Englehart. "I got two records to play."

"Delores, has the phonograph come?" asked Miss Martin.

"Darrell drove to town to get it," said Delores. "He'll be here any minute. Ruby's got 'Jingle Bells' and 'Silent Night.' "

Delores was to be Mrs. Santa Claus. She put on her mother's old black silk dress and a little lace cap of Grandma Wagner's. She stood in front of Teacher's mirror in the kitchen and rouged her cheeks and painted her lips. Then she peeped through a hole in the stage curtain, but Darrell wasn't there.

"Jeepers!" she cried. "There's Uncle Gustaf."

He hadn't said a word about coming. He had probably brought Christmas presents for everybody. He always gave her something nice. She wondered what it would be this year. Oh, it was exciting not knowing what anybody was going to give you.

Fernetta Sticklemeyer came out of Teacher's bedroom dressed as Mother Goose and Ruby Englehart as a fairy queen.

"My Mama went to Mobridge last week," Delores whispered to Fernetta. "She brought home a lot of packages and she hid them. I know right where they are — on the top shelf of Mama's closet."

"I got two records already," chimed in Ruby. "My uncle gave them to me."

"Go away," said Fernetta. "We're sick of hearing about those old records of yours. Who cares, anyway?" She turned to Delores. "What do you think is in them?"

"I shook one and it gurgled," said Delores. "Something runny."

Fernetta closed her eyes shrewdly. "Shampoo, maybe? Or a perfume set?"

"I hope it's perfume," said Delores. "But maybe it's for Lavina and not for me. Mama says I'm not old enough."

"She want you to stay a baby?" asked Fernetta.

Delores peeped through the hole again. "Why, there's Darrell. Look, Fernetta, he's talking to Katie Speidel and Norine Schmidt. I bet Uncle Gustaf brought them out from town. They're my best friends — in town, I mean."

Miss Martin sent Peter Hummel out to bring Darrell back of the curtain, but he had no phonograph. "The man wouldn't lend it without a down-payment," said Darrell, "and I didn't have any cash."

"Then you'll have to sing, children," said Miss Martin. " 'Jingle Bells' is the first number."

Hans and Fritz Holzhauer, Emil's older brothers, came to manage the stage curtain. They had graduated from the eighth grade several years before and liked coming back to their old school.

When everybody was ready, the program began. The curtains were pulled back on both sides, and the children sang

"Jingle Bells." Several recitations followed and then it was time for the play *Santa Claus at Home.* In the middle of the performance, Hans Holzhauer dashed back to the kitchen and said, "I'm having trouble. Where's a safety pin?"

"Go look on Teacher's pincushion," whispered Delores.

The curtain had come unhooked from the wire and was sagging badly. Hans hooked it up with a safety pin and the play went on. At the end, the curtains went shut without a hitch and everybody clapped.

After the program came the refreshments. The mothers were always willing to bring food to school, and all had contributed. Everyone ate candy and nuts, oranges and cookies. *Halvah* was popular. The Sticklemeyer family brought twelve pounds of the sticky, taffylike candy, all in one piece like a large loaf. Mrs. Sticklemeyer sliced off generous chunks and passed them out. Every child old enough to reach out a hand was eager for *halvah*.

"In the old days we made it ourselves," said Ruby Englehart's grandmother. "Now everybody buys *halvah* at the grocery store."

"What's it made out of, anyhow?" asked Uncle Gustaf Wagner. "Sunflower seeds? It tastes like machine oil to me."

The grown-ups laughed.

"Oh, it's got crushed sesame in it — that's a grain from the old country, and corn syrup, sugar, egg whites and vanilla," explained Grandma Englehart.

"Whatever it's got in it, it sure tastes good to me." Pete Hummel thrust a large bite in his mouth.

"Oh, not so fast!" cried Grandma Englehart. "That's not the way to eat *halvah*. My mother she make me eat it so — first a big bite of bread, then a little bite of *halvah,* then bread again. That way it goes not so fast. It's better for the stummick too."

The others laughed. The room was filled with warmth and friendliness, with good talk and laughter. The children were shrieking and romping with the school dog, Spike. Grandpa Englehart was telling a story:

"Never vill I forget! When I turned over that first strip of prairie sod, I remembered that no man had ever touched it before, since the day the good Lord had made it. I tell you then I vas a little scared — and that old Indian watching me too. Never vill I forget vat he said — just three words: 'Wrong side up.' Then he turned his back and walked away."

Nobody said anything. Suddenly the light in a lamp on the window sill flickered. A gust of wind blew in through the broken pane. The lamp flared again and went out. Mrs. Sticklemeyer screamed, and her youngest, little Alvin Calvin, ran to her and began to cry.

Pete Hummel quickly moved the lamp to a safer place. Then he went out the front door, and in a minute was back.

"Hey, folks!" he shouted. "We're gonna have a white Christmas all right. It's snowing hard."

"Snowing — no!" answered the women.

"Looks like a storm comin' up," Pete went on. "Guess we better be gettin' on home."

"Don't tell me it's goin' to be a blizzard," cried Mrs. Sticklemeyer. "I ain't got Adolph's red flannel underwear out yet!"

The others laughed nervously, getting up from their chairs.

"You can't go yet," said Miss Martin, trying to shout above

the din. "Santa Claus still has a little work to do. The children haven't had their presents. We drew names and . . ."

"Santa Claus! Santa Claus!" cried the children. "We want our presents." "What you got for us, Santa Claus?"

Emil Holzhauer, wearing his red suit and bearded mask, put his head out from behind the stage curtain and cried: "Hey, wait! Don't go yet. I ain't had my show. What you think we made this crepe-paper fireplace for? Don't you know I got to climb down the chimney and scare the little kids?"

Just then the curtain wire broke and came down. The dog, Spike, barked and pulled at it, and this time a safety-pin was no help at all.

"Come on, we gotta go home," called Pete Hummel again.

"Go home?" cried the women, startled.

Mrs. Englehart had a plate of cookies in one hand and a dish of nuts in the other. Mrs. Hummel was passing out fruit, and Mrs. Wagner was cutting another large three-layer chocolate cake. The refreshments were not half over.

Darrell jumped on a chair in the center of the stage. "Santa Claus hasn't come down the chimney yet," he shouted. "Wait a minute, please . . ."

But no one was listening.

Delores ran to her mother. "Don't let Papa go yet," she said, with her mouth half full of *halvah*. "We've had lots of snowstorms before and we always got home. I want to see what Jacob Sticklemeyer's got for me . . ."

But Delores could not stop her father. Johannes Wagner said in a loud voice: "There's a storm coming up. Better get home quick, folks."

"Can't we eat first?" cried the boys.

"Don't wait to eat," said Sam Englehart. "Take your food and go home."

"Leave the refreshments for Teacher!" laughed Uncle Gustaf.

"Oh no!" cried Miss Martin. "I'm going to Aberdeen for the holidays. Everything here will get frozen. Take the food with you. Take everything with you. Maybe some of you will take my canned goods, so it won't get frozen while I'm gone."

Like leaves scattering before a wind, the pleasant gathering broke up. Quickly the children thrust presents into each other's hands and in Teacher's. Dishes and food, wraps and small children were collected by the women. Caps, coats, scarves and four-buckle overshoes were hastily put on. Each family took a carton of Miss Martin's canned goods and everybody started to go, calling: "Merry Christmas! Merry Christmas!"

"I want a present from Santa Claus!" wailed little Christy Wagner. Minna wrapped him, screaming, in a blanket and Johannes threw him up over his shoulder.

"Delores, hurry now, get on your wraps. We're going," called Mama Wagner. "Ach, now, what is the matter? What are you crying for?"

"That crazy old Jacob, he didn't give me much — just a stationery, without even pictures on it," sniffed Delores. She opened the small box and showed the note paper to her two girl-friends from town, Katie Speidel and Norine Schmidt, who were waiting for Uncle Gustaf to come.

Miss Martin came running out into the hall and touched Johannes Wagner lightly on the arm. "Mr. Wagner," she said. "We're about out of coal . . . Do you think you could bring some? Before I get back?"

"Yah, yah, sure!" replied Johannes. "I see about it right away, quick, tomorrow. I been too busy to take care of it before."

"You going to town tonight, Miss Martin?" asked Mrs. Wagner.

"Yes," said Miss Martin. "Gustaf said he would take me. I'll leave everything as it is and throw a few things in a suitcase. I'll get the fast train to Aberdeen tomorrow."

Delores saw the worried look in Miss Martin's eyes fade away, as Papa promised to bring the coal. The girl tied her scarf tightly under her chin and buttoned her coat. Miss Martin was still standing there. She had her pretty blue silk dress on, the one she wore to church on Sundays, but no sweater, no wrap, and the front hall was cold with the door standing open. Impulsively, Delores ran to her and threw her arms about her.

"Good night, Miss Martin," she whispered. "Merry Christmas. I hope you have a nice vacation." She followed her parents out into the stormy night.

After the truck engine started, the cab was warm and shielded them from the wind. Only a little snow was falling, but it might get worse in an hour's time. As they rumbled away, Delores looked back and saw the lights in the schoolhouse. She was glad that Uncle Gustaf would drive Miss Martin safely to town.

"Will it be a blizzard, Papa?" asked Delores.

"What? This?" Papa Johannes laughed. "This is nothing."

◆ ◆ ◆

"Papa, you call this nothing?"

It was morning two days later. Delores ran down the steep stairs, through the cold front room and out into the kitchen. She was still in her bathrobe and carried her clothes over her arm. The furnace pipes did not reach to the upstairs bedrooms, and there was no stove, so she was cold. She pointed out the window, where the snow was beating against the house and a high wind was blowing.

"Jeepers! You call this nothing! *I* call it a blizzard."

"This is what Grandpa all the time talks about," said Papa, "the kind they had in the old days, back in 1910."

Darrell came in from the barn, snow-covered. "Here's a snowstorm for you, Delores," he said.

"I don't want it," said the girl. "Keep it for yourself."

Mama had a large frying pan full of sausage on the stove. It was sizzling and sputtering, filling the room with an inviting smell. Delores washed and dressed as quickly as she could. "Where's Christy?" she asked.

"I put him in the boys' bed downstairs," said Mama. "He don't feel so good. He cried all night, and wouldn't let me sleep."

Hearing his name, Christy came out of the bedroom and ran to his mother, crying. She took him up in her arms. Oscar Meyers, the hired man, came in from milking and sat down to eat. Then Darrell came up from the cellar with a coal bucket half full of coal dust.

"How can I shovel coal when there's no coal to shovel?" he demanded.

"I want coal, not that stuff," said Mama. "That's only dust. I got to have *coal* to burn in the kitchen stove."

"There's no coal left," said Darrell.

"No coal?" Papa looked dumbfounded. "Why, I trucked a big load all the way home from Firesteel just last month."

"In October that was," said Oscar.

"We been burning it for three months already," said Mama. "It can't last forever. That furnace is a big hog, the way it eats it up."

Delores said, "There's no coal at school either," but her father did not seem to hear her.

"Fine time to tell me we're out of coal," he shouted, "right in the middle of a big snowstorm. A fine time, I say."

"I've told you a dozen times, Johannes," said Mama, "but always you are too busy. What we going to burn now? The sideboard? Our dresser set we got for our bedroom when we was ten years married?" Mama Wagner was a good-natured woman, but her dark eyes flashed when she was angry. "Get me some wood. No wood — no dinner today."

Johannes ate his breakfast quickly and started toward the back door.

"Wake that lazy Phil up, Darrell," he said, "and you boys come on out. We'll get fuel all right, even in a snowstorm. You come too, Ozzie."

"You tear down the barn for fuel?" Mama called after them. As soon as the door closed, she looked at Delores and laughed. "Your Papa he know he should have got the coal long time ago. He is ashamed, but he won't admit it. It is fun to rub it in a little."

"What'll we burn?" asked Delores, lifting the stove lid. "This fire's going *out.*"

"Your Papa, he find fuel all right," chuckled Mama, "and

he find it quick, Ozzie will see to that. Get your coat and Christy's and put them on. Bring me my old red sweater."

Delores took Christy on her lap and put his coat on him. She looked out the window and showed him the snow coming down. She was glad it was vacation and she did not have to make the effort to get to school. After Christy jumped down from her lap, she slumped lazily in her chair.

What would she get for Mama for Christmas? She wanted something nice this year. But with all this snow, when would she be able to go to town? The snow wasn't coming *down* at all. It was coming sideways, straight from the north, pushed along by the wind. In some places the ground was swept clean. In other places, drifts were piling up against the farm machinery which stood in the barnyard. The wheels of the tractor were half-covered already.

"If the tractor costs so much money," asked Delores, "why don't Papa take care of it and put it in the barn? It's getting snowed under, and so are the plows and the drill and the disc and the drag and both the combines."

"How big a barn you think we got?" asked Mama. After washing up the dishes, she started preparations for dinner. "I was going to bake bread today, but how can I with no fuel?"

Christy ran to his mother and hung on her apron. He coughed and his nose was running.

"Hold him, Delores," said Mama. "Keep him out from under my feet."

Delores held Christy again. "Listen!" she said. The sound of sawing and chopping could be heard. "They're chopping, Mama."

"Ach!" laughed Mama. "The railroad ties — I thought so. We are lucky we have land on both sides of the railroad track, so we have plenty of ties. Sawing ties — that will be good exercise for a cold day."

Discarded railroad ties had been left along the tracks by the section men who kept the road in repair. In return for plowing a fireguard two furrows wide along the track, the farmers were allowed to take the ties. Johannes Wagner had hauled a large pile into the barnyard and unloaded them by the chicken coop. He intended to build a "tie shed" out of them, posts and supports covered with straw, for shade for the cattle in summer and protection from snow in winter. But now he had to use them for fuel.

The door soon opened and Darrell and Philip brought in big armfuls of chopped wood, sawed chunks of ties split for the stove.

"Make us a good hot dinner, Mom," begged Darrell.

"I'll think about it," said Mama.

"We had to shovel all the way to the chicken coop," said Darrell.

"Jeepers!" complained Philip. "No fun sawin' wood with snow blowin' up in your face." The boys hurried out again.

"Delores, you scrub the floor," said Mama. "I'll go down cellar and see if I can find something to eat. The cellar's so cold, I'm afraid my canned stuff will freeze."

Delores swished the mop over the linoleum and Christy crawled in the puddles of water she made. Mama came upstairs with a basket full of canned goods. She set the jars on the floor back of the stove.

"Make Christy stay out of the water, Mama," said Delores.

"Mama, take me up," screamed Christy. "Gimme candy. Buy me candy bar."

Mama picked the boy up and held him on her lap. She sat down in the kitchen rocker and rocked until he fell asleep. Then she put him back to bed in the side room again. At noon, she made macaroni salad, boiled potatoes and opened canned chicken. Papa and Oscar and the boys ate quickly and went out again. The house got colder and colder. There seemed to be no let-up in the storm.

In the afternoon, Chris Bieber appeared on his tractor, bringing cousin Reinhold Wagner. Reinhold was a tall, lanky town boy, sixteen years old, Uncle August's son. Uncle August ran a barber shop in town.

"I came to spend Christmas vacation on the farm," laughed Reinhold.

"You brought us a fine storm from town," said Delores.

Chris Bieber was a neighbor who lived two miles from the Wagners. "I was in town buyin' groceries," he said, "and I ran into Reinhold. He was crazy to get out to the farm, and his Pop wouldn't bring him, so I did." He turned to Mrs. Wagner. "Got any coal?"

"What? You folks out too?" Minna laughed.

"Vera Mae's been givin' me heck," said Chris. "I thought Johannes and I could take his truck to town and get some coal for both of us."

"Fine time you pick for hauling coal," grinned Delores.

"Where's the men-folks?" asked Chris.

"Out sawin' railroad ties," said Minna. "The furnace is out and the house is cold. No coal even for the kitchen range. We're burning tie wood today."

Chris Bieber laughed. "Reiny, guess we better go help."

By nightfall, the cellar had wood in it, and the downstairs was warm from a wood fire in the furnace. Even though he knew his wife, Vera Mae, would worry, Chris Bieber stayed all night, so he could help get the coal in the morning.

When morning came, it was still snowing. After an early breakfast, Johannes said: "Ozzie, you take the tractor and the hayrack and go out to the stacks and get a load of hay. Here's three big boys to help you. Clear the snow off one of the stacks and drive the range cattle down there to eat. Bring a load of hay back to the barn for the saddle-horses and milk-cows. Don't know how long this storm will last. Phil, you can drive the tractor part of the way for Ozzie. Reiny and Darrell, you'll have to shovel some."

"Oh boy! Shovel some? I'll say so," said Darrell.

"Yippee!" exclaimed Reiny. "I been dyin' to buck a few drifts."

"Criminy sakes!" growled Philip. "I'd like to stay in and keep warm. What we got a warm house for?"

"Come on, boys," called Oscar, opening the door.

"Can I go with the boys, Papa?" asked Delores. "I can shovel some."

"Nope, you stay in and help your Mama," said Papa. "You know how she gets in a storm like this. Try and keep her cheered up."

"Oh shoot!" cried Delores. "The boys get to have all the fun."

"Ain't you comin' with us, Pop?" asked Darrell.

"Nope, Chris and I are taking his tractor and my truck and

we're goin' after a load of coal," said Papa Wagner. "We got to load the truck with wheat, to hold it down on the road. No tellin' when we'll get back."

After the boys and men left the house, Delores was left alone with her mother and little brother.

"The men'll get in a ditch," sighed Mama, "and the boys'll never make it. The stacks are two miles away across the prairie. They'll have to shovel every inch."

"Don't you worry none," said Delores. "They'll make it all right."

The house was quiet now except for Christy's coughing. Delores went down cellar and filled the furnace with wood, then into the front room to listen to the battery radio. It was still cold there, with the northwest wind blowing around the corner. She had to put both coat and snowpants on to keep from shivering.

"You come out of that cold room," called Mama. "You'll catch cold."

"Just a minute," said Delores. "It's time for the news — maybe I can get the weather report. If it stops snowing, we'll go to town tomorrow and I'll do my Christmas shopping."

The radio sputtered, but the battery was not dead. Delores could hear what the man was saying:

" . . . bad storm over the Great Plains . . . from Nebraska to Montana . . . cattle and sheep drifting before the storm . . . huddled in fence corners beneath the drifts . . . miles from their home ranges . . . wet snow . . . freezing on their eyes, ears and bodies . . . many reported dead . . ." That was all. It faded out again.

Alarmed, the girl ran to the kitchen.

"The cattle are freezing to death," she cried. "The man said the drifts are getting so high they are burying the cattle and they can't get out."

"Ach! So!" cried Mama. "That must be north of here, up in Canada."

"He said in Nebraska," replied Delores. "That's south of here."

"Nebraska!" exclaimed Mama. "They always get bad blizzards in Nebraska. I always read it in the paper."

"We better put our cattle in the barn, Mama," said Delores, "before they freeze to death."

Mama laughed. "How big a barn you think we got, hey? First you put all the farm machinery in, and now seventy head of range cattle. What you think? You talk like a dumb town girl."

"Don't they get cold staying out all winter long, with no food and no shelter?" asked Delores.

"Some of them die," said Mama sadly. "One winter they all died — three thousand dollars we lost. Plenty farmers lose their whole herd. Even if they live through the winter, they're poor skinny creatures by spring." Mama brought out her sewing basket and a pile of clothes to mend.

"If the hay lasts out," she said, "they'll live. That is, if they can get to the stacks. In a storm like this, they start going with the wind at their backs, and they keep going till they get stopped by a fence and get banked up against it, or till they all get drowned in a creek. The Herefords are the best ones to nose the snow away and try to eat the prairie grass underneath, like the horses do. The others got to get to the stacks." Mama sewed quietly, then she added, "When summer comes, they eat grass again and grow strong."

"I don't see why Pop couldn't let me go out," said Delores. "I'm stronger'n Darrell is. I can throw him wrastling."

"You'd go off and leave me here alone?" said Mama. "Go get your embroidery and do a little work on it."

Delores brought out her dresser scarf, replaced the embroidery hoops, and started to work on the design of wild roses.

"Jeepers!" she cried impatiently. "My thread always gets knots in it."

Mama did not answer. Her face looked sad. The needle and thread in her hand went steadily up and down. The kitchen grew dark as the afternoon wore on. Christy was sleeping on the bed in the next room. He stirred restlessly and began to cough. Mama put down her mending when she could no longer see.

"Light the lamp, Delores," she said. "Did you clean the chimney?"

"Criminy, no," said the girl. "I forgot."

"Go do it quick then."

Delores washed the blackened lamp chimney and polished it with a dry, clean cloth.

"It gets dark early in a storm," said Mama. "Is plenty oil in all the lamps?"

"Yah, I filled them full," said Delores. "Now if we had electricity —"

"If we had electricity," Mama interrupted sternly, "we would have no light at all. The people in town have no lights when the storms come. Lavina tells me so, and Grandma

Wagner and Mrs. Thiel and all the ladies. In town they sit in darkness till the storm is over. They eat cold food and sit in a cold kitchen. Electric stoves do not burn wood." Mama got up and put more wood on the fire.

"I wish we had a pretty little house like Grandma's just the same," said Delores. She jerked her embroidery thread impatiently.

Mama sighed. "The house must wait — so your Papa says. The farm machinery must first be paid for. Last year a new tractor and a new truck too. All this machinery, it eats up all the money."

"Why do we buy so much?"

"Oh, the men — the men, they put their heads together, they say they got to have more and more."

Delores looked out the window. "Everything's white," she said. "I can't see a thing but a white blur. Blizzards are so white."

"Except when they are black," said Mama.

"Black!" said Delores. "Whoever heard of a black blizzard?"

"I have *seen* one," said Mama. "I have seen plenty of them and tasted them too."

She went into the bedroom to look at Christy. She put her hand on his head, and came back, shaking her own.

"The baby is sick," she said, "and at a time like this."

"What's a black blizzard?" asked Delores.

"Sand, dirt, gravel blowing up and hitting you in the face instead of clean snow," said Mama, sitting down in the rocker. "You are too young. It was before you were born, in the thirties — 1935, 1936 and 1937."

"Oh, the dust storms," said Delores. "We studied about

them in school. But I didn't know they happened here. I thought they were in Kansas and Nebraska."

"Yes, and here too, in the Dakotas," said Mama. "The wind don't stop at the state line. They were all over the Great Plains from Texas to Montana. The Sioux Indians say the prairie grass should never have been broken up. Maybe they are right. Maybe the first settlers shouldn't have broken the sod and planted big fields of wheat. When so many dry summers came in a row, the wind blew day and night and whoof — the air was full of dirt. It blew in our eyes, our noses, our throats, our lungs. Many died of tuberculosis, children too. Ach! The hard time, the trouble, the sickness . . . five years in a row we made no crop . . . not a blade of wheat came up. Ach! it was terrible . . ." Tears came in Minna Wagner's eyes, as she looked out the window.

"I don't like the snow," she said. "I don't like the wind. But whenever I see a white blizzard blowing, I thank God it is not a black one." Christy began to cough in the bedroom. "Bring him to me," said Mama.

Delores carried the boy out and put him in his mother's lap. Christy, usually so full of life and spirit, was limp and sickly now.

"He's had fever all day," said Mama. "And on such a day we run out of coal and have a cold house."

"The boys — why do they stay so long?" said Delores. "Soon it will be dark."

"In warm weather, they can chase the cattle down to the stacks," said Mama. "But now the stacks are covered with snow. They must shovel all that long way."

"Does Christy need a doctor?" asked Delores.

"All summer, all fall, we run to town two-three times a week for nothing at all," Mama said. "All summer, we go twice a week to take you kids to the show. What is a show when a baby lies sick of the fever?"

Delores stood beside her mother, looking down at her little brother.

"So many times we run," Mama went on, "we use gas, we have the old car, the truck, the tractor. We can take one or the other and run off to town. We can run in after supper and get home before bedtime. Nine miles — it is nothing. But in the winter time, when the big blizzard comes, and the baby lies sick, there is no car to take him to the doctor."

"The old car — it's broke down," said Delores.

"Oh yes, the old car, it's broke down, it's got a flat tire, it's got this and that wrong with it," said Mama, "and the truck and the tractor, they are gone."

The tears ran down Mama's cheeks, and Delores could not bear to see it. She wanted to cheer her up but she did not know how.

"What for? What is all this machinery for?" There was despair in Mama's voice. "Always more and more machinery to get out of order, to break down when we need it most. The men are not farmers any more. They are mechanics, and poor ones at that."

Delores got up and put more wood on the stove.

"Maybe Christy will be better tomorrow," she said. "What'll we fix for supper?"

"I'm making sour *knipfla,*" said Mama. "Are the potatoes done?"

"Yah," said Delores, trying them with a fork.

"The roll of dough is ready," said Mama. "Take the scissors and cut little pieces off and put them into the potato-and-water mixture. Let it cook till the *knipfla* get done. Then I'll put the sour cream and vinegar in."

Suddenly a rush came against the outside door. The dog, Rover, barked and a scuffle was heard. The door burst open, and in rushed the three boys, followed by the hired man.

"Shut the door! Shut the door quick!" called Delores. "Brush that snow off outside."

"Jeepers!" cried Darrell. "It's nice and warm in here. My cheek's frozen. Let me get it thawed out." He brought in a panful of snow and held handfuls up to his cheek.

"Did you get some hay?" asked Mama, as she put Christy back to bed.

"No," said Oscar. "Pretty big job gettin' hay in weather like this."

"Got stuck a dozen times," said Phil. "Had to unhitch the hayrack and leave it out there. Maybe we can drive the cattle up to it tomorrow and let them eat."

"Tractor was always gettin' stuck and we had to dig it out," said Reiny.

"The snow blew up in our faces and then froze," said Darrell. "We had to stop and pull the ice from our eyes and warm our hands on the exhaust from the tractor. We couldn't see the road ahead of us."

"Jeepers!" exclaimed Delores. "Wish I could have been out. You guys have all the fun."

"Fun?" cried Reiny and Philip. "It was work and we're hungry."

"Go take off those wet clothes," said Mama, "then we'll eat. We won't wait for Papa. No tellin' when he'll get here."

"Why is it so quiet?" asked Darrell. "Where's Christy? Where's my little pal? I want to have a boxing match with him."

"He's a pretty sick boy," said Mama, pointing to the bedroom.

"Jeepers!" Darrell shook his head. "What a Christmas vacation!"

◆ ◆ ◆

When morning came, Delores ran to the window the first thing. "Well, I'll be jiggered," she said, "if it ain't still blizzarding."

"A peach of a snowstorm for you, Delores!" cried Darrell at breakfast.

"This one's yours, not mine," retorted Delores.

"If only the wind would die down," said Cousin Reinhold, "we could go out and play Fox-and-Geese."

"Go find an Eskimo to play with," said Delores. "Criminy sakes, but the house is cold."

"Where's Pop and Chris Bieber?" asked Darrell.

"Ach! They never got back at all," said Mama. "All night I could not sleep one wink. What if they ran in a ditch and got buried deep in the snow?"

"Big strong men can dig themselves out," said Oscar Meyers.

"Darrell, go build up the furnace fire," said Mama. "That tie wood burns out overnight. That's why it's so cold."

Reinhold stepped out on the back porch and came quickly in again. "Golly! It's twenty-seven below," he said.

"Jeepers!" exclaimed Phil, shivering beside the stove. "Twenty-seven degrees too cold for me. Zero's bad enough."

"And tomorrow's Christmas," sighed Delores. "A fine Christmas it will be. No presents, and Mom without sugar and cake flour to make a cake."

"I wasn't gonna fix much," said Mama. "I thought we was goin' in to Grandma Wagner's. But even if Christy was well, we could never get there now."

Delores stood by the window. "If it would just stop snowing . . . we could go after all. Then if the stores were still open . . ." She remembered she hadn't bought a thing for Mama for Christmas.

"We'd better forget about it," said Mama. "If we get coal for Christmas, we'll be lucky. And Pop back safe. That'll be Christmas for me."

After breakfast, Oscar and the boys went out to tackle the haystacks again. Delores went into the front room and turned on the battery radio. She listened a while, then came back to the kitchen. She sat down and began to work on her embroidery.

"Mama, the man on the radio told how to signal for an airplane."

"Airplane!" said Mama with scorn. "With such contraptions I will have nothing to do. The tractors — they give us enough trouble. All they do is break down."

"Teacher is not afraid of airplanes," said Delores. "She took a ride with Paul Kruger in his plane once. He flew her all the way from town out to Oak Leaf School after the Fair. She said she felt like she had wings on, herself!"

Mama shook her head. "Such foolishness!"

"The man said a big circle or a plus-sign tramped in the snow would signal a plane to land here," Delores went on. "He said to make an F for food, and a double XX for doctor or medicine."

"All foolishness," said Mama. "What good to make a sign when the wind blows like sixty and covers it right up?"

"He said to spread ashes," replied Delores. "I can go in the cellar and shovel some . . ."

"Delores Wagner!" exclaimed Mama. "Are you then so dumb? Who of us is starving? Are we then out of food? Look at all the eggs. Look there back of the stove at all my jars of canned stuff. Are we then starving?"

"No, not yet," said Delores hastily. "But we're out of sugar, and you said you used the last of the coffee this morning. Other people are out of food. One family had only macaroni to eat for three days, because they couldn't get to the store. They got sick and tired of it."

"Poor sort of people," sniffed Mama, "if they had no home-canned stuff and no root vegetables in their cellar."

"He said all their meats and vegetables were in frozen food lockers in town," said Delores. "And they couldn't get to town."

"Frozen food lockers," sniffed Mama. "Such new-fangled notions. What's the matter with their own cellar?"

"But you had to bring all our stuff up from the cellar, to keep it from freezing," said Delores. "Over the radio, they told about a man who froze to death and the snow covered his body. Just his feet were sticking out. They had to bring a bulldozer to dig him out of the snow."

"Ach! Tell me not such awful things, when Johannes has been gone so long," wailed Mama.

"The airplanes are dropping bales of hay to the cattle, and they are taking sick people to the hospital," Delores went on. "I bet if Paul Kruger knew . . ."

"Who of us is freezing or dying?" asked Mama. "Only Christy has a sore throat. You think I don't know how to take care of him? Let the airplane go to those who are in need."

But by noon, Mama herself was worried. Christy was not getting better and she had used up all the medicine. She brought the little boy out and held him in her arms in the rocking chair. "If only I could get that prescription filled, and some more cough medicine . . ."

"I wish we had a telephone," said Delores. "We could call Paul Kruger up and ask him to bring it out."

"The farmhouses are too far apart for stretching telephone wires," said Mama. "If Darrell was here, he could go on Nellie. All the coffee is gone and there are only a few matches left . . ."

"The cattle wouldn't get their hay, if the boys went," said Delores. "Why can't I go to town? I can ride better than Darrell."

"You? A little girl like you?" cried Mama, horrified. "Every year we read in the paper about little girls getting lost in the deep snow. You think I'm crazy enough to let you go?"

"Now Mama, don't be silly," said Delores. "The radio says the worst of the storm is over. You know the first three days of a storm are always the worst, and this is the third day. Uncle Rudolph would be out to his farm today, Mama, doing his chores. He comes out every other day about one o'clock to feed his cattle. It was storming so bad esterday, I don't suppose he ever came. He'd be sure to come today."

Mama nodded, but did not say anything.

"If I could get over to Uncle Rudolph's barn," said Delores, "I could go to town with him in his jeep."

"Are you crazy, girl?" cried Mama. "How you gonna get there, anyhow?"

"Ride a horse," said Delores. "Old Nellie's got plenty sense. She won't go where it's not safe. It's no worse than riding to school. If it was school you'd *make* me go."

It took a lot of coaxing. Only because Christy was getting worse did Mama finally consent. "I'll let you go as far as Uncle Rudolph's," she said.

"O.K., Mama," said Delores. She ran to get ready.

"You put on two pairs of jeans under your snowpants," said Mama, "and a sweater under your coat. Get a wool scarf for your head."

"Oh, Mama, you'd like to dress me up like an Eskimo," laughed Delores. "You'd think I was making an expedition to the North Pole. I'm not Admiral Byrd. It's only four miles to Uncle Rudolph's."

"Four miles in a storm is twice as far as in fair weather," said Mama. "If you see smoke at the Hunstad's place, stop there and rest."

"Yah, Mama. Sure." Delores started out the door, with the doctor's prescription and grocery list in an inside pocket.

"You'll be lucky to find Uncle Rudolph there," said Mama.

"If he's not, you turn right around and come home. I'll send Papa to town after he comes with the coal."

"I hate to leave you alone, Mama," said Delores.

"Pooh! You go along, you!" Mama tried to laugh, but her eyes were wet.

Delores was glad to get out, even if the snow was still blowing and the wind icy cold. It was better than being cooped up inside. She shoveled a drift away to get into the barn. Sugar nickered and wanted to go, but Delores knew the larger horse, Nellie, would be better. When she came out of the dark barn on Nellie's back, she had to squint because the snow was so bright. Over in the east the sky looked lighter.

It took a long time to get to Uncle Rudolph's. After crossing the railroad track, Nellie chose her own path, walking where there was least snow, often up to her belly. When the drifts became deeper, Delores got off and led the horse, kicking a path with her feet. The wind swept across the prairie with terrific force, and she was glad she had worn so many clothes. But walking was not easy for her or for the horse.

"Jeepers!" she said to herself. "At this rate, it will take me all day."

At last she came within sight of the Hunstad place, a small farmhouse with a windbreak of trees, on the banks of Oak Creek. Smoke was pouring from the chimney, which meant that the hired man must be staying there to look after the cattle. She knew that the Hunstads lived in town in the winter. It was too hard to lead Nellie all the way to Uncle Rudolph's. Delores wondered if she could leave her in the Hunstad's barn. She went to the back door and knocked.

The hired man, nicknamed Whiskers, opened the door a crack, and peeped out, unshaven, with a pipe in his mouth.

"Yah, yah!" he nodded in answer to her question. "Sure mike! That's O.K. Put your horse in the barn. It makes me no difference out."

He did not notice that the girl was cold. He did not ask her to come in, or offer to help. The kitchen door was quickly closed to keep the heat in and the cold out. Delores had no chance to say that she would like to come in and rest awhile.

She managed to get the barn door open, and found an empty stall and some oats for Nellie. It was only a mile now to Uncle Rudolph's. She could make better time without the horse. If she could only catch Uncle Rudolph there, doing his chores . . . She hated to think what she would do if he was not there. There was no house at his place, only a barn and straw shed.

The mile was long and the snow in Oak Creek valley was deep. The girl trudged wearily on. Uncle Rudolph's barn was a long way from the road which circled a hill. It stood in a low flat place near a bend in Oak Creek. She walked faster. After the sun came out, the snow blinded her, and she could not see which way she was going.

Ach! There he was! She could see Uncle Rudolph's jeep by the barn and his cattle under the straw shed. How happy she felt. A jeep could go anywhere, even on drifted roads. How lucky! Had he just come, or was he ready to leave? If he was leaving, could she ever catch him? Would he see her waving or hear her call? If she missed him, she would have to walk to town, five more miles. She tried to run and stumbling, fell headlong. She lay there for a minute, resting, then pulled herself to her feet.

She saw a man come out of the barn and she knew it was Uncle Rudolph. He was just going away in his jeep. She called and waved frantically. The jeep started, then it stopped. It started up again, and this time, turned and came toward her. Just as she had hoped, Uncle Rudolph had seen her. He came as close as he could, then stopped and waited till she came up.

"What's the matter?" he asked. "Where you goin'? Anything wrong?"

"Christy's bad sick," said Delores. "I got to get medicine at the drugstore in town. Pop's haulin' coal and the boys are gettin' hay, so there's no one to go but me. Will you take me in the jeep?"

"Sure as shootin'," said Uncle Rudolph. "Pile in."

It was better luck than Delores had hoped for. She gave a sigh of relief. The jeep rocked her from side to side, but being shaken up was better than walking. The jeep had side-curtains too, which kept off the wind. It had chains on all four wheels, so it crawled over snowbanks four and five feet high. It moved slowly but surely and at last reached Yellowstone Trail, where other cars had left tracks. From there on, the going was easy. But because of the late start, it was nearly dark when they reached town.

"You stay at Lavina's tonight," said Uncle Rudolph. "I'll pick you up at the trailer-house first thing in the morning and take you home."

Delores hurried to the grocery. The streets were emptier than she had ever seen them. The snowplow had pushed high banks of snow into the gutters. The sidewalks had not been shoveled, but were tramped down in a narrow path. Delores bought coffee, matches and five pounds of sugar at the grocery first, then just got into the drugstore before it closed. She had Christy's prescription filled and bought a bottle of cough syrup. By the time she came out, the other stores were closed. In Holzers' window she saw a beautiful nut-cracker set, a wooden bowl with nut-picks and a cracker. She looked at it longingly, but could not get in to ask the price.

"Oh, dear," she thought. "Now I haven't got a thing for Mama for Christmas."

The lights shone brightly from the little blue trailer-house, and were a sign of welcome as the girl came stumbling up the street through the snow. She pounded on the door and Lavina opened it.

"Criminy sakes!" cried Lavina. "First Pop, then you — on a day like this. Where did you drop from — out of an airplane?"

"Uncle Rudolph brought me in his jeep." Delores dropped her packages and sank on the couch, exhausted. For a while she could not talk. "I got a pain in my side," she whispered.

"Here, drink this cup of coffee," said Lavina. "You look white as a sheet. This will warm you up inside and rest you."

Lavina had a good supper ready and after Delores had eaten, she felt better. Melvin came in and Delores told them her whole story. "Now tell me about Pop," she said.

"Pop stopped in after he got his coal loaded up," said Lavina. "He and Chris Bieber had dinner at Grandma's. I knew you folks would never be able to get into Grandma's for Christmas tomorrow, so I bought some groceries for Mama and a little Christmas tree. Grandma sent over her Christmas treats for all you kids."

"You started out to our place?" asked Delores.

"Yah, twice, but had to turn back," said Lavina. "Mel was afraid of the roads. I tried to find Paul Kruger with his airplane, to take the stuff out, but they said he was bringin' a sick woman in to the hospital."

"Mama won't have anything to do with airplanes," said Delores. "She says they break down as easy as tractors."

"Oh, Mama!" laughed Lavina. "She's always the last one to catch onto a new style. Remember her bobbed hair? We'll get her in an airplane yet. Boy! Was I ever glad to see Pop. What do you think? *He* bought a box of groceries for Mom too — the very same stuff I bought. I made him take everything out on his coal truck, but he went off without the Christmas tree."

"I'll take it," said Delores, "and then we'll have a tree — at least."

Delores slept soundly with Lavina's twins. On Christmas morning, she was stiff all over and felt very tired, but Uncle Rudolph came to the door early. She drank a cup of coffee and ate a piece of summer sausage for her breakfast. She put her bundles and the little evergreen tree in the back of the jeep, then climbed in.

It was a beautiful Christmas day. The blizzard was over and the sun came out in all its brilliance, to make the snow shine and sparkle. Uncle Rudolph took Delores as far as the Hunstads, then hurried back to town to have Christmas with his family. At the Hunstads, the girl put her groceries in a feed sack and tied the Christmas tree to her saddle. She did not go into the house and Whiskers, the hired man, did not come out. She rode across the prairie, following her path of the previous day, where it was still visible.

"Here comes our Christmas tree girl!" Mama met her at the door and gave her a tight hug.

"Lavina sent the tree, Mama," said Delores. "Ain't it pretty?"

"Ach! You are home safe again," said Mama. "I was sick with worry when you did not come home last night. Poor Christy, he could hardly breathe. I ran the steam kettle all night for his cough. I never once took my clothes off even."

"I got the prescription filled just before the drugstore closed."

"Good," said Mama. "Soon he will be better."

"Jeepers! Is the house ever hot!" exclaimed Delores. "Must be, Papa brought the coal."

"Yah, at last," said Mama. "They got stuck three times and had to walk back to town to get Schweitzer's wrecker to come pull them out. They took half the load over to Biebers, so Vera Mae could have a warm house for Christmas too."

"And the boys?"

"They finally got a load of hay to the barn, and the cattle came in," said Mama. "Poor kids — that is work for men, not for boys. That Ozzie, he's only nineteen — just a kid too."

"Mama!" exclaimed Delores, remembering. "Papa's got to get coal for school too."

"Yah, I told him," said Mama, "and he said there is plenty time for that."

"He better not wait too long," said Delores.

Soon Papa and the boys came tramping in.

"Merry Christmas!" shouted Papa. "They tell me it's Christmas!"

While Mama was preparing and roasting the duck for Christmas dinner, Delores set the little evergreen tree on the sideboard in the front room. Darrell hung shiny balls and tinsel on it. Mama brought her packages out from their hiding place and laid them under it. After dinner, Mama got Christy out of bed and held him on her lap to see the tree. Delores heated the iron and pressed her wild rose dresser scarf. It was all she had to give to Mama.

"Jeepers! Is the house ever hot!" cried the boys.

Once the lignite coal in the furnace was well started, it made the house too warm. The family threw off sweaters and coats.

"It's like summer, hey?" Papa chucked Mama under her double chin.

"Come on, let's open the presents," begged the boys.

"What Santy Claus bring me?" asked Christy. "Candy bar?"

The gurgling package was perfume, just as Delores expected. She got a new blue sweater and a pocketbook too. Mama gave her a kiss for the dresser scarf, and said wild roses were her favorite flower. Ozzie and the boys got plaid wool shirts and Christy a toy dump-truck. After admiring all the presents, they all ate *Kaffeekuga* and drank hot coffee.

Then came Grandma Wagner's treats — a paper sack for each grandchild which contained one orange, one apple, nuts, cookies, Russian peanuts, a candy bar and a popcorn ball. Grandma sent a new tie for Papa Johannes and for Mama a pretty pincushion crocheted on the wishbone of a chicken.

At the last minute, Papa tossed a small box into Mama's

lap. When Mama opened it, they all gathered round and gasped in astonishment. It was a pretty gold wristwatch on a gold-chain bracelet.

"Well, I never!" exclaimed Mama. The kiss she gave Papa was a resounding smack. "Look at me here now, with this! A wristwatch! Don't that beat the Dutch! And I thought I was lucky to get *coal for Christmas!*"

Kapugen

Jean Craighead George

A wolf howled. He began on a note lower than a bear's growl, then climbed the scale to the highest pitch of the wind and held it there.

The cry traveled across the snowy tundra and was heard by a young girl standing at the door of a small green house. The wooden structure sat on the edge of an Eskimo village on the bank of the frozen Avalik River in Alaska. She pushed back the halo of fur that framed her lovely face and listened. The wolf was telling her to come with him. She did not answer.

Julie Edwards Miyax Kapugen knew the wolf well. He had shared food with her when she had been lost on the endless tundra. He had run and played with her. He had rested in her tent while she had nursed him back to health from his bullet wounds. Now he was trying to locate her. He must not find her. He must go away, far away. After many years of separation, Julie was going home to her father, Kapugen, and he, she knew, would kill the wolf.

"That is how it is," she whispered to the howler. "If you

come near Kapugen, he will shoot you. He is like all Eskimo hunters. He will say, 'The wolf gave himself to me.' "

The howl rose and fell.

Julie squinted toward the distant caller. "Stay away, beloved Kapu. I am going home."

She waited. The wolf she had named Kapu after her father, the great hunter and leader, did not call again. Quickly she opened and closed the first door that led into Kapugen's house. She walked into the qanitchaq, an entry room designed to keep out the cold. Its walls were hung with parkas and boots, and on the floor stood paddles, guns, and gasoline cans. She put down her pack, took off her sealskin parka and maklaks, or boots, and hung them on pegs. She stepped to the second door, which opened into the living room, and hesitated.

She thought of her childhood on the Eskimo island of Nunivak in the Bering Sea, and of her maidenhood in Barrow on the Arctic Ocean. Then she thought of the day she had left that town desperate to end an arranged marriage. She had gone out on the tundra planning to walk to Point Hope and take a boat to San Francisco to meet her pen pal, Amy. On the tundra wilderness she had become hopelessly lost.

She tried not to think about the lovable wolf pack that had felled a caribou and saved her life. She must put them in the past. She had found her beloved father and was going home to him.

Yesterday he had welcomed her in this very house. Her heart had lightened and her burden of loneliness had fallen away. Her head had danced with joyful thoughts.

Her happiness had not lasted long. Within a short time she had realized Kapugen was not the same father who had taken her hunting and fishing with the seasons on Nunivak.

He was not the father who had lived in grace with the sea and land. Kapugen had changed. He had a white-American wife, a gussak. He had radios, a telephone, and a modern stove. Julie could have accepted these things had not her eyes fallen on Kapugen's airplane pilot helmet and goggles. She had seen them on the man in the airplane window who had shot Amaroq, the magnificent leader of her wolf pack. This she could not reconcile. When Kapugen had left the house, she had put on her pack and returned to her camp along the barren river.

There, alone in the crackling Arctic night with the hoarfrost spangling her tent with ice ferns, she knew she must return. No matter what he had done, Kapugen was her father, and she loved him.

"We do not judge our people," she heard the Eskimo elders say, and Julie pointed her boots toward Kapugen.

Now, only a wooden door stood between them.

She opened it and stepped inside. Kapugen was home. He was seated on a caribou skin on the floor sharpening his man's knife. He was alone.

He did not look up, although Julie knew he had heard her enter. She tiptoed to the iglek, a pile of furs stacked into a couch almost as tall as she. She climbed up on it, sat, and folded her hands in her lap.

Kapugen sighted along his knife to see if it was satisfactorily sharp. Julie picked a thread from her woolen sock. Kapugen selected a section of bearded-seal hide and cut a slender thong from it. He tied the thong around his boot. Julie sat quietly.

Presently Kapugen looked out the window at the marine-blue sky of the sunless winter day.

"The wind has died down," he said. "That is good."

"The stars are bright," Julie added.

"That is good," said Kapugen.

A silence followed. Kapugen tightened the boot thong and at last looked at her.

"Did you hear the wolf?" he asked, looking into her eyes.

"I heard the wolf," she answered.

Another silence ensued. Kapugen did not take his eyes from her eyes. Julie knew he was speaking to her in the manner of the Eskimo hunter who communicates without sound. His eyes were saying that a wolf did not give that call of friendship very often.

Julie did not answer. She studied her father.

Kapugen was a stocky man with a broad back and powerful arms. His face was burned brown from the Arctic wind and sun, and his hands were blackened by frostbite. His hair was shorter than she remembered, but his chin was still smooth and plucked hairless. A faint mustache darkened his upper lip. He sat with his legs straight out before him.

"The wolf knows you." He spoke slowly and thoughtfully.

"He does," Julie answered.

Kapugen picked up the seal hide and cut another thong. Julie waited for him to speak again. He did not. He gave his knife one last hone and put it in the sheath on his belt. In one movement he rose to his feet and opened his arms. She jumped down from the iglek and ran to him.

After a long, comforting embrace, Kapugen lifted Julie's chin and touched the smooth olive skin of her cheek.

"I'm glad you came back," he said. "I was afraid I had lost you for a second time. I love you with the fullness of the white moon."

"That's a lot," she said shyly. He crossed his feet and lowered himself to the caribou skin, then patted it and invited Julie to sit. Julie saw the question on his face. She answered it.

"I broke the marriage arrangement with the son of your serious partner." Her voice was very soft.

"If a man and a woman," Kapugen said in a low, even voice, "do not love, they part company. That is the right way."

They sat quietly.

Kapugen, Julie saw, wanted to know more about her past, but, respecting her privacy, he did not ask. She must tell him no matter how painful her memories were.

"Do you not know," she asked in her gentle voice, "where I've been since that day Aunt Martha took me away from you to attend school?"

"I only know you went to Barrow when you were thirteen and old enough to marry," he answered, pacing his words slowly. "I happened to meet Nusan, your mother-in-law, in that town. She said you had run off and died."

"That was a terribly sad thing for her to say when she didn't really know," Julie said. "I am sorry. I will try to tell you what happened — perhaps not all — some things are still too sad."

Julie told him about her unhappy life in Mekoryok, the town on Nunivak, her days in Barrow, her marriage, and how deeply she feared Daniel, her angry husband. She recounted her days on the tundra with the gentle wolf pack and its kind leader, Amaroq, but she could not bring herself to say that Kapugen had killed him. The words would not form.

When she was done, Kapugen lowered his eyes for a moment, then looked up at her. His eyes said how much he loved her and how grateful he was that she was alive.

Julie buried her head on his shoulder, and he hugged her against his strong chest. This time as he held her, she felt forgiveness run up her spine and into her heart and mind. Kapugen, after all, was a provider for his family and village. Eskimo providers hunted.

"I am very tired," she finally said, her shoulders slumping. Kapugen brushed a strand of hair from her forehead. He lifted her in his arms, carried her to the iglek, and placed her upon it. She sank down into the sweet, soft furs and pulled a grizzly-bear skin over herself.

"I am glad you came home, Miyax," he said, and kissed her. She smiled to hear him call her by her Eskimo name. Like most Eskimos, Julie had two names, English and Eskimo — Julie Edwards and Miyax Kapugen. Hearing her father call her Miyax made her feel closer to him, and she decided she would let only him call her that. The name bound the two of them to her mother, who had given it to her, and to each other. To the rest of the people she would be Julie.

She closed her eyes and slept deeply.

"Good morning, Kapugen. Good morning."

Julie sat straight up in her furry bed and looked around. The man's voice was loud and crackly, but there was no one in the room. Kapugen came out of the bedroom.

"Good morning." He spoke to the glittering CB radio on the bookshelf. "Good morning, Atik. Good morning." Julie recognized the name of the hunter she had met with his wife, Uma, and baby on the frozen Avalik River. Astounded to hear him in the room, she slid off the iglek and sat on Kapugen's caribou skin, watching the radio and listening intently.

"Good morning, Malek," said a woman's voice. "Good morning."

"Good morning, Marie. Good morning."

For almost an hour the villagers of Kangik awoke and greeted each other on their CBs. Their voices filled the darkness of the sunless morning with cheer.

Ellen, Kapugen's wife, came out of the bedroom and, seeing that Julie was awake, greeted her.

"Good morning, Miyax," she said.

"Julie," she said softly but firmly.

"As you wish," said Ellen, and turned her back to dip up tea water from a thirty-gallon plastic container. There was no running water in frozen Kangik.

Julie studied Ellen. Her bright-red hair with its strange curls was an oddity to her, as were her pale eyes and eyelashes. Julie found herself staring and wondering about her father's new wife. When breakfast was over, she climbed up on the iglek and watched Ellen at her desk. She wrote in a book, glancing up at Julie now and then as if to ask if she was all right. Julie said nothing.

Next Ellen read a book. When lunchtime came around she even cooked by looking at a book. In the early afternoon Ellen phoned her mother in Minnesota.

"Hello, Mom," she said. "I have a daughter." She smiled and glanced at Julie.

"Yes, she's pretty," Ellen said. "Beautiful smooth skin and big almond eyes. Her hair is as black and shiny as polished ebony." Embarrassed, Julie slid back under the grizzly fur and peered at her father's wife over the ruff. She wondered how this woman had gotten so far from home and why she did not go back.

"Want to say hello to my mom, Julie?" Ellen asked.

She did not answer. Julie knew English perfectly. Briefly she had forgotten it after Amaroq had been killed, but now she understood every word being said. She just did not feel like talking to Ellen.

Julie had been terribly disappointed to discover her father had taken a wife from the outside. To the Eskimos there are two peoples — the people within the circle of ice and the people outside it. Ellen was not from within. She moved and talked too swiftly. Her voice was harsh, and she laughed loudly like the jaeger seabirds.

Julie slowly adapted to her new life. She washed dishes and cooked fish and caribou meat for Ellen. She scraped skins and prepared them for the market, and she chopped ice in the river and put it in the container to melt.

She read Ellen's books when Ellen was out. Her English schooling in Nunivak had been excellent. She read the books avidly, eager to learn about the outside world. From time to time when no one was around, she would walk along the river and listen for her wolves. Once she heard Kapu, and looking around to see if Kapugen was outside, she cupped her hands and howl-barked a warning. Kapu replied with silence. He had gotten the message.

One day while Julie was scraping a bearded-seal skin to make boots, a new voice came in over the CB.

"Good morning, Kapugen. Good morning."

"Good morning, Peter Sugluk," said Kapugen. "You are back, are you?"

"I am back, all right," he said. "And I am picking up two

qivit sweaters Marie asked me to bring to you." Julie recalled Uma telling her that the women of Kangik knitted sweaters and scarves from the warm, featherweight underfur of the musk ox. Kapugen, she had said, sold these incredibly warm clothes to merchants in Anchorage and Fairbanks for enormous prices, many hundreds of dollars.

"Come on over," said Kapugen, and turned to Julie. "Peter Sugluk is my business partner's adopted son," he said.

"He speaks with a strange accent," said Julie.

"It should not be strange," said Kapugen. "He speaks Yupik like we do, not Iñupiat like the people of Barrow and Point Hope."

The Eskimo language has two branches. Yuk, or Yupik, is spoken in southwestern Alaska and Siberia. Inuk, or Iñupiat, is spoken across northern Alaska, Canada, and Greenland. Julie had learned Yupik in Nunivak and Iñupiat in Barrow. Although she understood Peter, who spoke Yupik, she could not place his accent. She wondered where he came from.

Presently there was a rap on the inner qanitchaq door.

"Come in," called Kapugen, and Peter Sugluk stepped into the warm room.

"Good morning, Kapugen," he said, and glanced at Julie. "You must be Julie. Good morning." His smile was beguiling and friendly.

Julie looked up at a bronze-faced young Eskimo. He was tall. His nose was straight, his cheekbones high, and his eyes were bright half-moons under dark brows. He wore a tunic of reindeer over close-fitting leather trousers. His maklaks were of polar bear, trimmed with sled dogs in black-and-white calfskin. Ermine tails with black tips danced along the trim of his sleeves and boots when he moved. He looked old to Julie, perhaps eighteen or nineteen as compared to her fourteen, going on fifteen, years. She looked down at her sealskin and went back to her scraping.

"What they say is right," she heard Peter say. "You are beautiful."

Julie went on working. She did not want to be known for her beauty, but for her wisdom and fortitude, Eskimo virtues. She did not look up until he opened the door and was gone, but she thought she had seen him tap a toe and raise his palms in the dance symbol of celebration.

Two weeks passed. The days became turquoise blue as the earth tilted into the sun. By the time the bloody red ball came over the horizon on January twenty-second, Julie felt comfortable in her new home and village.

One day when Ellen was teaching at the school and Kapugen was at the desk poring over papers, she put down her work and stood before him.

"Aapa," she said softly, "I have been gone a long time on the tundra and I have been deep in a dream world with the wolves. Now I am awake. What can I do to help you?"

"That is good, all right," he said, looking up at her. Noticing that she was studying the papers he was working on, he spoke.

"These papers are the records of our musk oxen. Malek, Peter, and I keep track of them for the bank in Fairbanks. The bank finances our industry."

"Industry?"

"All Eskimo villages are corporations now," Kapugen said

rising to his feet. "Unlike the American Indians, who live on reservations under government supervision, we run ourselves like a business. Our people own stock in the village corporation and share the profits." This did not make sense to Julie, but Kapugen seemed to think it was important, so she listened. "The Kangik Iñupiat Corporation is pretty big, all right," he said, pointing to numerals in the book. "We have a musk-ox business, a construction company, a store, and an electrical-generator company. We also get money from the oil taken from our land." She still did not comment, so Kapugen stood up and took her hands.

"Miyax, you must learn to hunt."

"I can hunt," she answered. "I can trap ptarmigan and snowshoe hares."

"You must learn to shoot a gun," he said. "We need you. Kangik is almost a deserted village. Many of the houses are empty, all right. The caribou have not circled back to us for two years, and the people are hungry. Many have moved to Wainwright and Barrow."

"That is too bad," Julie said.

"We are suffering," he said. "That is how it is." Kapugen went into his bedroom. He returned with a .22 rifle and cracked open the barrel.

"Is there really so much hardship in Kangik?" Julie asked. "I met your friends Uma and Atik up the river. Uma said that the people of Kangik make lots of money knitting musk-ox qivit into mittens and sweaters. She said you are raising musk oxen to help your village; and that you are a great leader."

"Uma is cheerful," Kapugen said, and smiled. "She was raised to admire a leader no matter what he does."

"I understand that," Julie said softly.

"You do, all right," he said, and looked at his helmet and goggles. "You do, all right," he repeated. Kapugen's face told Julie that her father now knew that the wolf he had shot from his plane was her friend. He looked very unhappy.

"Food is scarce in Kangik," he said, hastily changing the subject.

"Can't you fly your airplane and get gussak food for the village?"

"When the caribou fail to return, no white man's food can keep us healthy."

"The fish?" she asked.

"We also need flesh and fat to survive in the cold," he answered. "And nothing tastes so good as the caribou and the whale."

Julie smiled. "That is true."

Kapugen slipped several bullets into the .22 and put on the safety so the gun could not be fired. He handed it to her. They went into the qanitchaq and put on their warmest clothing. Kapugen picked up his bear rifle. He put the carrying strap around his neck and rested the gun on his back. When Julie was dressed, he opened the door. The cold air sucked the breath from their mouths and swirled snow in their faces.

The sun was just rising, although it was ten o'clock. The rosy light illuminated a dip in the landscape that was the frozen Avalik River, and beyond it the huge platter that was Kuk Inlet. But for the village, a cluster of little wooden houses on pilings that kept them from melting the permafrost, all else was barren tundra.

Julie glanced at Kangik and held her breath. The village, which had seemed so vibrant on that first night she had laid eyes on it, was plain and dreary. Several of the houses were packing boxes in which snowplows and trucks had been shipped to the villages along the Arctic coast. Many were boarded up and deserted.

A dull murmur caught her attention.

"What is that?" Julie asked. "I hear it often at night."

"The electric generator," Kapugen said. "It runs on gasoline and makes electricity for our radios and stoves and lights."

The humming generator, sounding like a sleeping bear, gave a strange kind of life to the still, cold village. Julie listened for another sound. A dog barked once, a door squealed as it swung on its hinges, and a voice called out. The sounds were swallowed by the subzero cold. She listened more intently. There was no sound from Kapu.

Kapugen signaled her to follow him, and they walked east on the river ice in the somber polar light. After a short distance they both stopped and watched the sun light up the treeless, blue-green snow.

"You will like Ellen, I think, all right," Kapugen said after a while. Julie did not answer.

They went on up the river. Their footfalls smashed the ice into snow. It squeaked like glass, swirled up, and fell softly, making a trail of powder behind them. The sun had rolled along the horizon for almost an hour, and now it was setting. Kapugen turned to Julie.

"We will hunt foxes," he said. "Some live near the musk-ox corral. Watch what I do. I learned to hunt in my father's boot steps. It is the best way."

Julie stepped in his boot tracks and followed him off the river ice onto the tundra. The ice fog that had arrived with the dawn began to thicken.

After a short hike Kapugen opened a gate, and he and Julie entered a large corral. Dark boulderlike forms loomed in the blue fog. Eleven musk oxen stared at them. Small clouds of frozen breath hung above their heads.

A wolf howled. Julie looked at Kapugen in alarm.

"The hunt is over," he said. "The foxes hide when the wolf howls."

"Ee-lie, Kapu," Julie whispered to the wolf, "stay away, stay far, far away."

Kapugen and Julie walked home.

Ice fog erased the landscape, and it was many days before Julie and Kapugen returned to the corral to hunt foxes again. They walked through a galaxy of sparkling ice crystals that floated over the quiet tundra. Kapugen led, and Julie stepped in his tracks.

After a long walk Kapugen stopped. He fixed his eyes on a distant spot, and Julie followed his gaze. A figure appeared and disappeared and reappeared like starlight on water.

"Lift your gun," Kapugen whispered. "When the fox stops moving, put the bead of the front sight into the notch in the rear sight. Click off the safety and pull the trigger slowly."

Julie fired and missed. Kapugen walked on, turning his head from right to left as he scanned the snowscape. His gun was slung across his back parallel to the ground; his hands were grasped behind him. He was alert to the most subtle movements and faintest sounds. Kapugen hunted like a wolf, and like a wolf he knew when there was no game. He stopped in the corral to check the uminmaks.

As he turned to go home, he kicked back the snow. It was not very deep, the wind having stripped the flat tundra of snow and exposed the grasses and sedges. For this reason the Arctic tundra was a perfect home for the grass-eating, well-garbed musk oxen. The tip of Kapugen's maklak touched an ancient ground birch that was only seven inches high. He leaned down. Around it grew bilberry, Labrador tea plants, and a few dwarf willows.

"The uminmak's favorite foods," he said to Julie, then looked at the plants more carefully. "They have been eaten too close to the roots. The oxen are running out of wild food."

"The grasses are taller outside the fence," Julie said. "Why don't you let them roam free?"

"So we can gather the qivit easily," Kapugen answered. "And," he added with bluntness, "so the wolves will not kill the oxen."

Julie felt a flush of blood run through her. She closed her eyes and swallowed hard.

"Soon," Kapugen said, "I must fly to Barrow to buy alfalfa pellets for the uminmaks. They need more food." He walked on. Julie placed her feet in his boot tracks.

"A white fox hide," Kapugen said turning to her, "brings fifty dollars in Fairbanks."

"Fifty dollars," Julie repeated to herself, and looked back toward the village. For the past seven months she had thought about no one but herself and her wolves. For seven long months she had directed all her thoughts inward toward staying alive. Now, as she walked behind her father, she knew it was time to become an Eskimo again, a person who helps the family and the village community.

She would not miss the next fox.

Julie not only followed Kapugen, she looked where he looked, she sniffed the winds he sniffed. When he stopped and listened, she stopped and listened.

A ptarmigan burst out of the snow and vanished behind the ice cloud it had created.

"How much do they give for a ptarmigan?" she asked.

"Ten dollars," said Kapugen. She thought of the huge polar bear she had seen in Barrow. His great white hide must be so valuable, it could feed all of Kangik.

"How much do they give for nanuq?" she called above the wind.

"Nothing," replied Kapugen. "Only the Eskimos can harvest nanuq, the great white bear, and we cannot sell him. He gives himself to us. We give him to our people. That has always been so." Julie nodded.

They arrived at a three-sided shelter in the musk-ox corral. Snow was drifted high around the sturdy structure of heavy plywood. It was roofed with corrugated steel.

"This is where we put the hay and pellets for the umin-maks," Kapugen said. "It keeps the food from being buried under the drifts."

He looked up and smiled. Julie looked up too. A solitary bull was running toward them. She glanced at her father. Kapugen did not seem alarmed, and sure enough, when the bull was only a few yards away, he stopped. He ogled them. Shreds of qivit trailed from his shoulders.

The bull was massive but not very tall. He barely came

up to Kapugen's chest. His huge neck muscles formed a hump on his back that was higher than his head. His tail was remarkably short, his hair so long it swept the ground like a skirt. His feet were enormous ice choppers. A bold boss of horn, curved tips pointed forward, met in the middle of his forehead like a helmet. The chunky rocklike animal bore a strong resemblance to the woolly mammoths of the past. He snorted.

"One of the last old-time animals," Kapugen said. "White men say he is a goat-antelope. To the Eskimo he is uminmak, the animal born to the ice and the wind and the snow." Kapugen held out a bilberry stalk to him. "Once," he went on, "there were millions of uminmaks in northern Alaska. When the Eskimo got guns, they shot them all. Every one.

"The U.S. government tried to bring them back. They got thirty-three calves from Greenland and set them free on Nunivak in 1930. When that herd was large, they brought some calves to Fairbanks and later set them free. We have a few wild ones on the North Slope now.

"The government helped me bring bull and cow calves to Kangik to start a qivit industry."

The bull snorted and pawed the ground, then rubbed his head against his foreleg.

"Is he angry?" Julie asked.

"He is rubbing a gland near his eye on his leg. The scent from the gland warns the herd. It is not musk, as the white man calls it. It smells fresh and clean, like snow."

"What is he afraid of?" Julie asked.

"He is prey," Kapugen said. "He is concerned about all things; you, me, our guns, and the odors on the wind."

Kapugen sniffed and squinted into the glaring snow. "He is saying the grizzly bear is awake."

"The grizzly bear?" Julie asked.

"Aklaq awakened last week in a warm spell," he said. "She has two yearling cubs and they are hungry. She has been staying close to the musk oxen, all right," he said. "That is not good. Like the wolf, the grizzly can kill an uminmak. Uminmak is smaller than a bear and not very bright."

Kapugen cupped his hands behind his ears.

"The herd is coming," he said, and smiled proudly. Out of a bright spot of ice glare the other musk oxen appeared, rolling along as if on wheels and seemingly pushed by the wind. They were a sturdy, well-knit group. The beasts slowed down, hesitated, then, circling like a whirlpool, forced the yearlings and calves into the center of their group for protection.

"They are alarmed," said Kapugen, looking around.

"The bear?" Julie asked, afraid that he was going to say wolf.

"I do not know," he answered.

The herd was quite close, and Julie could see the difference between the males and the females. The females were smaller, and their horns did not meet on their brows, as did those of the males. Both sexes had large eyes that protruded from their heads several inches. With these eyes they could see to the sides, the front, and the rear, and they could see in the dark as well as in the painful light of ice glare. The uminmaks are creatures honed by darkness, sun, and intense cold.

Kapugen moo-grunted.

A female left the group and came toward him. She hesitated when she saw Julie. Kapugen walked slowly up to her making soft sounds. When she was close, he reached out and scratched her head.

"This is Siku, Miyax," he said. "I found her on the tundra. Her mother had just been killed by a wolf pack. Siku was moving inside her. I opened the belly and lifted this little musk ox onto the ice — the siku; then I wrapped her in a caribou skin and took her home.

"I fed her on a bottle, and she lived and gave me the idea to raise musk oxen."

"Is it hard to raise them?" Julie asked.

"Not too hard," Kapugen replied. "Once, not too long ago, when the caribou were scarce, the people of Kangik, Wainwright, and Barrow raised reindeer. Malek was a herder. I met him and told him of my dream. He came to Kangik to join me. The state of Alaska gave us several more oxen to go with Siku. In time we had a herd and gathered qivit." Julie reached slowly out and touched Siku. The large eyes rolled her way, but the cow did not move.

"Siku," he said, laughing and rubbing her head roughly. "You started it all." She snorted and went back to the herd. The uminmaks had broken their fortress circle and were cropping grass.

"How many musk oxen do you have, Aapa?" Julie asked.

"Four bulls and seven females and yearlings. Not many, but the herd is growing. There will be four little calves in May or June if the wolves do not get them." He looked directly into her eyes.

Julie did not speak. She was thinking of that day on the tundra when an airplane came out of the mist and, with the burst of gunfire, killed Amaroq, the intelligent and kindly leader of her wolf pack.

She turned away from Kapugen's gaze. He was telling her he had killed the wolf to protect these musk oxen. He was thinking of his people, his eyes said, and they added that he would do it again if he had to.

Julie was terrified for Kapu and his pack. Wherever the caribou were, she fervently hoped her wolves were with them.

The sun, which had been up for two hours, was now sinking behind a horizon of ice mist. It glowed sparkling red, then disappeared. The long polar twilight entombed the top of the world as Julie and Kapugen turned homeward. In the short time it took to walk back to the village, the temperature dropped ten degrees. The wind gathered force. Kapugen pulled a bit of underfur from his parka ruff, wetted it, and held it up in the gale. It bent and froze in a hook.

"The wind is from the west," he said. "Tomorrow ought to be still and clear."

He pushed back his dark glasses and looked at the sky. "If the wind doesn't change in the night, tomorrow I will fly to Barrow."

"To get food for the uminmaks?"

"If I have time. Tomorrow I must take my wife to the doctor."

"Is Ellen sick?" she asked tentatively.

"She is pregnant," Kapugen answered, and smiled so broadly his teeth shone white even in the dark twilight.

Pregnant, Julie thought. A child would be born. She was both pleased and not pleased. The very thought of a baby stirred warm feelings within her, but she also knew she had found her father only to lose him again. She walked along in silence. Distant barks sounded in the purple dusk.

"The dogs," said Julie. "I often hear them bark. Are they yours?"

"I have a team," he said.

"But you have snowmobiles," Julie said. "You don't need a team."

"I have snowmobiles," he answered. "But I love the dogs."

"I love the dogs, too," she said, thinking of the wonderful animals who were descendants of the wolves.

North of the town they came to a large Quonset hut. It faced a flat windswept plain that was covered with a long sheet of steel chain.

"Airplane iglu," Kapugen said, pointing to the hangar. Here her father's airplane resided. "Airplane runway," he added, gesturing to the metal-mesh landing strip. "I must check out the plane for tomorrow. Do you want to see it?"

She really didn't. She did not want to see that airplane from which the fatal shots had come — ever. She still felt the pain of Amaroq's death. Inside that iglu were the wings of a father she did not know.

She took off her mitten and reached into her pocket. There she kept the totem of Amaroq she had carved to hold his spirit after his death. She clutched the totem and felt better.

"Coming in?" Kapugen asked.

"I'll keep hunting," she said. "A ptarmigan will bring ten dollars, and you can buy food for Siku."

"I have a treasure for you in there," he said, pointing to the Quonset with a broad smile. Julie drew back. She did not want to see that airplane.

"I have ermine," he said, reaching out for her hand. "Beautiful glistening white ermine. They are for you to make something regal for yourself." His eyes told of his love for her. "Come see them. They are in a box by the door. I was going to sell them to the furrier in Fairbanks, but when you came back to me, I wanted to wrap them around you. They are yours."

Kapugen opened a small door in the big door of the Quonset and held it for Julie.

"I must learn to hunt," she said, drawing away. "I will bring you a fox or a ptarmigan. Later I will come see my treasure." She smiled and backed around the corner of the Quonset. Kapugen went inside and closed the door.

A wolf howled.

Julie shut her eyes and wished that tomorrow would be clear and windless so the metal bird would take Kapugen and Ellen to Barrow. A day alone would give her an opportunity to call her wolves and tell them to go far away from the hunter who would protect his oxen at all costs.

The Hungry Old Witch

Charles J. Finger

She was a witch, she was very old, and she was always hungry, and she lived long ago near a forest where now is Uruguay, and just in the corner where Brazil and Argentina touch. They were the days when mighty beasts moved in the marshes and when strange creatures with wings like bats flew in the air. There were also great worms then, so strong that they bored through mountains and rocks as an ordinary worm makes its way through clay. The size and the strength of the old witch may be guessed when you know that she once caught one of the giant worms and killed it for the sake of the stone in its head. And there is this about the stone — it is green in colour and shaped like an arrowhead a little blunted, and precious for those who know the secret, because he who has one may fly through the air between sunrise and sunset, but never in the night.

The old witch had another secret thing. It was a powder, and the knowledge of how to make it was hers alone and is now lost. All that is known of it is that it was made from the dried bodies of tree-frogs mixed with goat's milk. With it she could, by sprinkling a little of it where wanted, make things grow wonderfully. She could also turn plants to animals with it, or change vines into serpents, thorn-bushes into foxes, little leaves into ants. Living creatures she also changed, turning cats into jaguars, lizards into alligators, and bats into horrible flying things.

This old witch had lived for hundreds of years, so long indeed that the memory of men did not know a time when she was not, and fathers and grandfathers and great grandfathers all had the same tale to tell of how she had always devoured cattle and pigs and goats, making no account at all of carrying off in one night all the animals of a village. To be sure, some had tried to fight her by shooting arrows, but it was of no use, for by her magic the shafts were bent into a shape like a letter V as soon as they touched her. So in time it came about that men would put outside the village in a corral one half of what they had raised in a year, letting the old witch take it, hoping that thus she would leave them in peace.

At last there grew up a lad, a sober fellow of courage, who said little and thought much, and he refused to take animals to the corral when the time came for the old witch to visit that place.

When the people asked him his reason for refusing, he said that he had had a dream in which he saw himself as a bird in a cage, but when he had been there a little while a sweet climbing vine had grown up about the cage and on this vine was a white flower which twisted its way in between the bars. Then, as he looked at it, the flower changed to a smiling maiden who held a golden key in her hand. This key she had given to him and with it he had opened the door of the cage. So, he went on to say, both he and the maiden had gone away. What the end of the dream was he did not know, for at that point he had wakened with the sound of singing and music in his ears, from which he judged that all turned out well, though he had not seen the end of it.

Because of this dream and what it might betoken he said that he would not put anything in the corral for the old witch, but instead would venture forth and seek her out, to the end that the land might be free from her witcheries and evil work. Nor could any persuade him to the contrary.

"It is not right," he said, "that we should give away for nothing that which we have grown and tended and learned to love, nor is it right that we should feed and fatten the evil thing that destroys us."

So the wise men of that place named the lad by a word which means Stout Heart, and because he was loved by all, many trembled and turned pale when the morning came on which he took his lance and alone went off into the forest, ready for whatever might befall.

For three days Stout Heart walked, and at last came to a place all grassy and flowery, where he sat down by the side of a lake under a tree. He was tired, for he had walked far that day and found that slumber began to overtake him. That was well enough, for he was used to sleep under the bare heavens, but with his slumber came confused dreams of harmful things which he seemed to see coming out of the ground, so he climbed into the tree, where he found a resting-place among the branches and was soon asleep.

While he slept there came to the side of the lake the old witch, who cast her basket-net into the water and began to fish, and as she fished she sang in a croaking and harsh voice this:

"Things in the air,
Things in the water —
Nothing is fair,
So come to the slaughter."

They were not the words, but that is what the words meant. But unpleasant as was the song, yet it worked a kind of charm, and things came to her, so that her basket-net was filled again and again. The fish she cast into a kind of wicker cage, of which she had several.

Soon the croaking song chased sleep from the eyes of Stout Heart, and looking down he saw the wrinkled crone and the great pile of fish that she had cast on the bank, and his heart was grieved for two things — one that there was such waste of good life, the other that he had left his spear hidden in the grass. He grieved too, a little, because he knew that on account of his long walk he was weak from hunger and thirst. So there seemed little that could be done and he sat very still, trusting that until he was better prepared for action the old witch would not see him.

But all his stillness was of no avail. Looking at the shadow of the tree as it lay upon the surface of the water, she saw the lad's shadow. Then she looked up and saw him. Had she had her magic green stone with her, things would have been far different and this tale all the shorter. But not having it and being quite unable to climb trees, she said:

"You are faint and hungry. Come down, come down, good lad, for I have much here that is good to eat."

Hearing that, Stout Heart laughed, knowing that she was not to be trusted, and he told her that he was very well indeed where he was. So she tried another trick, spreading on the grass fruits and berries, and saying in a wheedling voice:

"Come, son, eat with me. I do not like to eat alone. Here are fresh fruits and here is honey. Come down that I may talk with you and treat you as a son, for I am very lonesome."

But Stout Heart still laughed at her, although, to be sure, he was a lad of great appetite and his hungriness increased in him.

"Have you any other trap set for me?" he asked.

Hearing that, the witch fell into a black and terrible rage, dancing about and gnashing her teeth, frothing at the mouth and hooking her long nails at him like a cat, and the sight of her was very horrible, but the lad kept his heart up and was well content with his place in the tree, the more as he saw her great strength. For in her rage she plucked a great rock the size of a man's body from the earth where it was sunk deep, and cast it at the tree with such force that the tree shook from root to tip.

For a moment the old witch stood with knit brows, then she went on her hands and knees and fell to gathering up blades of grass until she had a little heap. All the time she was cursing and groaning, grumbling and snarling like a cat. When she had gathered enough grass she stood up and began to sprinkle a grayish powder over the grass heap, and as she did this she talked mumblingly, saying:

"Creep and crawl — creep and crawl!
Up the tree-trunk, on the branch.
Creep and crawl — creep and crawl!
Over leaf and over twig.
Seek and find the living thing.

Pinch him, bite him, torture him.
Creep and crawl — creep and crawl!
Make him drop like rotting fruit."

So she went on, moving about in a little circle and sprinkling the powder over the grass. Presently the pile of grass began to move as if it hid some living thing, and soon the grass blades became smaller, rounded themselves, and turned brown. Then from them shot out fine hair-like points which became legs, and so each separate leaf turned to an ant. To the tree they scurried and up the trunk they swarmed, a little army marching over every leaf and twig until the green became brown, and louder and louder the old witch screamed, waving her arms the while:

"Creep and crawl — creep and crawl!
Up the tree-trunk, on the branch.
Creep and crawl — creep and crawl!"

The nearer to Stout Heart that they came, the louder she shrieked, leaping about and waving her long-taloned hands as she ordered:

"Seek and find the living thing."

Then Stout Heart knew that trouble was brewing indeed, for against so many enemies there was no fighting. For a time he avoided them, but for a time only, and that by going higher and higher in the tree, crawling along the branch that hung over the lake, but nearer and nearer the ants came, and louder she bade them to

"Pinch him, bite him, torture him."

At last there was nothing for it but to drop out of the tree, for he had been hanging to the end of a branch and the ants were already swarming over his hands and some running down his arms. So he let go his hold and went into the lake with a splash, down out of the sunshine and into the cool green-blue of the waters. He swam a little, trying to get out of the way before coming up, but had to put his head out soon to get a breath. Then suddenly he seemed to be in the middle of something that was moving about strangely, and it was with a sudden leaping of the heart that he found himself in the old witch's basket-net being drawn ashore. To be sure, he struggled and tried to escape, but it was of no use. What with her magic and her strength he was no more in her hands than is a little fish in the hands of a man. He was all mixed up with other lake things, with fish and with scum, with water-beetles and sticky weed, with mud and with wriggling creatures, and presently he found himself toppled head foremost into a basket, all dazed and weak. It was dark there, but by the bumping he knew that he was being carried somewhere.

Soon he was tumbled into an evil-smelling place and must have fallen into a trance, or slept. Again, he may not have known what passed because of the old witch's enchantments, for when he came to himself he did not know whether he had been there for a long time or a little. But soon he made out that he was in a stone house and through a small hole in the wall saw that the place where the house stood was bare of grass and full of great gray rocks, and he remembered his dream and thought that it was all very unlike what had really happened.

But in that he was not altogether right, for while he was in no cage and no twining vine with glorious flower was there, yet there was something else. For after a little while a door opened, and he saw standing in a light that nearly blinded him with its brightness a maiden full of winning grace, and light and slender, who stretched out her hand to him and led him out of the dark into a great hall of stone with a vast fireplace. Then having heard his story, which brought tears to her blue eyes, she opened a lattice and showed him a little room where he might hide.

"For," said she, "I also was brought to this place long ago, and when I came the old witch killed one who was her slave before me. But before she died she told me the story of the green stone which the witch has, and also how were used the magic powders. Since then I have been here alone and have been her slave. But now she will kill me and will keep you for her servant until she tires of you, when she will catch another. And so it has been for many, many years, and each one that dies has told the power of the green stone to the other, though none had dared to use it."

Now hearing all that, Stout Heart was all for running away at once and taking the maiden from that dreadful place, but just as he opened his mouth to speak there came to their ears the voice of the old witch.

"Hide then," said the maiden, "and all may yet go well. For I must go to get the green stone by means of which we may fly. With you I will dare. Alone I was afraid to venture."

Even then he hesitated and did not wish to hide, but she thrust him into a little room and closed the door. Through the wall he heard the witch enter and throw a pile of wood on the hearth.

"I have a new prize," said the ogress. "You I have fattened long enough and now you must be my meal. One slave at a time is enough for me, and the lad will do. Go then, fetch pepper and salt, red pepper and black, and see to it that you lose no time, for I am hungry and cannot wait."

The girl went into another room and the witch fell on her knees and began to build a roaring fire. Soon the maiden reentered, but running lightly, and as she passed the old woman she cast on her some of the magic powder which she had brought instead of salt and pepper. The hag had no idea that it was the powder that the girl had thrown, and thinking that she had been careless with the salt and pepper began to scold her, then getting to her feet took her by the hair, opened the door of the little room in which Stout Heart was, and little knowing that the lad was there cast her in, screaming:

"Stay there, useless one, until I am ready to roast you."

The maiden thrust the green stone into the hands of Stout Heart and at once they flew through the window and out under the arch of the sky. As for the old witch, the powder did its work and she began to swell so that she could not pass out of any of the doors. But presently the boy and girl, from a height at which they could see below them the narrow valley and the witch house, saw that the old hag was struggling to get out by way of the roof.

The two lost no time then. They flew swift and high. But swift too was the witch. Her growing had finished and out over the top of the house she burst, and seeing the escaping pair, began to run in the direction they had taken.

So there was much speeding both in the air and on the earth, and unlucky it was for the two that the green stone allowed those who carried it to fly only in the daytime. All this the maiden told Stout Heart as they flew. The old witch well remembered that at night there was no power in the flying stone and was gleeful in her wicked old heart as she watched the sun and the lengthening shadows. So she kept on with giant strides and leapings, and going at such a rate that she was always very nigh under the two in the air. No deer, no huanaco could have bounded lighter over the ground than she did, and no ostrich could have moved swifter.

When the sun began to drop in the western sky, and he and she were looking at one another with concern as they flew, the maiden bethought her of a plan, and scattering some of the magic powder on the earth she rejoiced to see that the leaves on which the powder fell turned into rabbits. The sight of that the witch could not resist, and she stopped a moment to catch some of the little animals and swallow them, so a little time was won for the fliers.

But the hungry old witch soon went on and regained the time she had lost and was under them again, running as fast as ever. So more powder was scattered, this time on some thorn-bushes, which changed to foxes. Again the old woman stopped to eat and the two gained a little. But the sun was lower and they found themselves dropping ever nearer to the earth, flying indeed but little higher than the tree-tops, and as they saw, the old witch in her leaps lacked but little of touching them.

Ahead of them was the lake in which Stout Heart had been caught, the waters red as blood with the light of the western sky, but the power of the stone was failing with the waning day, and of the powder they had but a small handful left. As for the witch, so near was she that they could hear her breathing, could almost imagine that they felt her terrible claws in their garments.

On the bank of the lake the last handful of the magic powder was cast, and they saw the grass turn to ants and the stones to great turtles as they passed over the water, but so low that their feet almost touched the surface of the lake. The power of the stone was growing weak.

The old witch, seeing the turtles, stopped to swallow them, shells and heads, and that gave the youth and maiden time enough to reach the opposite shore, where the power of the stone was quite exhausted as the sun touched the rim of the earth. The gentle maiden clung to Stout Heart in great fear then as they saw the old witch plunge into the lake, for she could travel on water as fast as she could on land. Indeed, the fearful old woman cut through the waters so swiftly that a great wave leaped up on either side of her, and it was clear that before the sun had gone she would have her claws in the two friends.

But when she was in the middle of the lake the weight of the turtles she had swallowed began to bear her down. In vain she struggled, making a great uproar and lashing her hands and feet so furiously that the water became hot and a great steam rose up. Her force was spent and the turtles were like great stones within her, so she sank beneath the water, and was seen no more.

Great was the joy of the people when Stout Heart brought the maiden to his home, for she became his wife and was loved by all there as the fairest woman among them.

The Feed Mill

Walter D. Edmonds

Tom drove up to Boonville with Polly Ann next morning. It was one of her days for doing housework. Drew took his time on the long uphill grade between the river bridge and the canal, for he was getting to be an old horse. But he brisked up on the level going and came down to Mill Creek and on up the grade to the railroad crossing at a ringing trot. Coming into town, where there were other horses, to say nothing of dogs and people, seemed to put some ambition back in him.

Polly Ann pulled up beyond the depot. The mill was on the right, standing below the railroad embankment with Mill Creek running underneath. Four stories high, the first walled in limestone, the other three in clapboards weathered gray, it was almost as high as it was long. Enormous tall, it looked to Tom, thinking of Breen's barn, which had seemed big when he saw it with Birdy. Under the fourth-story window in the peak was a sign lettered white on a black ground:

ACKERMAN & HOOK
FLOUR AND FEED MILL
Est. 1831

He got down from the spring wagon and told Polly Ann that he would walk home, whether he got a job or not. She looked down at him a moment, her mouth working a minute before it got to smile. Then she touched Drew's rump with the whip and rattled off up the street to her day's work. Glancing up at the sign once more Tom turned down the narrow road to the mill.

A team and wagon was drawn up beside the loading platform and two men were dumping feed bags into the box.

"You looking for somebody, son?" one of them asked. His overalls were thick with grain dust and Tom figured he must be one of the mill hands.

"I'm looking for a job," he said. "If there is one."

"Well, sonny, you'll have to ask the boss. In the office."

The man tilted his head in the direction of a one-story projection at the front of the mill.

Tom looked and was embarrassed to see that there were steps leading up to a door which had "Office" painted on it; he had walked right by without even knowing it was there. He walked back, climbed the steps, lifted his hand to knock, and hesitated.

"Walk right in," the man yelled from the loading platform.

So Tom put his hand on the knob and with a kind of chill coming up his legs and the small of his back, turned it and stepped inside.

It was a smallish square room with plain board walls. A

large round station stove stood against the left-hand wall with a door beside it leading into the mill. Opposite, two windows looked out against the green slope of the railroad embankment, but the sun was high enough now to shine down into them. At a table between them two men were playing checkers. Both turned to look at Tom when he came in and the younger one got out of his chair and came around to the counter where the high brass cash register was and pulled out a pad of order slips, asking, "What can we get for you today, my boy?"

That embarrassed Tom even more. He took his hat off, though both the men were wearing theirs. He started to clear his throat, but that turned out to be difficult, too, and when he did get his voice operating, it came out scratchy and high-pitched and he made himself repeat.

"I came to see if I could get a job here, mister."

He guessed that the older man with his white hair and bristly white beard must be Erlo Ackerman so the other would be George Hook, but he was afraid of misnaming them until he made sure.

"Well," said the man at the counter, "what would your name be?"

"Tom Dolan."

"How old are you, Tom?"

"Going on fourteen," Tom said, which was true enough and sounded better than thirteen.

"That's pretty young for a feed-mill job."

The old man's words came out with his breath. It gave them a rough, almost harsh sound, even though his voice was mellow.

"Now, Erlo," the younger man said. "How old were you when you come to work here the first time?"

So now Tom was sure which man was Erlo Ackerman.

Erlo was looking up under his eyebrows at something on the wall back of Tom. Tom turned to look, too. It was a three-foot piece of polished dark walnut with letters which had been picked out with gold paint carved into it. They read:

THIS MILL OPENED FOR BUSINESS
THIS DAY
August 22, 1831

His eyebrows, which were bushy and black, in contrast with his white beard, came down again, and Tom saw the shrewd eyes looking through them at him, like a badger's behind underbrush. But then he saw Erlo's mouth twitch a little underneath the beard.

"I was twelve, going on thirteen, George. As you well know. But there wasn't the business then there is now. Not enough to wear a boy down." He cleared his throat with a hawking sound and cast his eye towards the white china cuspidor in the corner, but he didn't use it. "But as you also know, George, I came out of a hardworking family." His eyes fastened on Tom's then. "If you're Tom Dolan, your pa must be Nob Dolan."

Tom saw the meaning behind that and felt the blood rush up into his head.

"Yes," he told Erlo, "Nob's my pa, but we ain't seen anything of him in eleven years. We get along without him. He wasn't much use afore he left, anyway." Then he straightened his back, facing both men. "And if it comes to that my grampa wasn't much for doing work, either. Ma's the only one who's ever worked hard in our family. I figure it's time I got a job, too."

"I didn't go for to rile you, son," Erlo Ackerman said. He rubbed his hand across the top of his brow, as if he was squeezing his memory. "Seems your gramp must have been Chick Hannaberry, Tom; but I don't remember which of his girls married Nob Dolan."

"Polly Ann," Tom said.

"Polly Ann," Erlo said, and nodded. "I remember her, now. Not much more than mouse high, George. Pretty girl, too."

His breath went in and out with a rough sound. Tom supposed old men might find breathing harder than when they were young. He didn't say anything; it didn't seem like a proper time to do so, with the old man rustling around with his thoughts and memories, mumbling to himself something about "a scalawag, that Chick was," half a-grin. And then he seemed to pull himself together. "Tell you what, Tom. We'll see what you can do for a week, eh? If it works out, then we'll keep you on."

He looked up at George Hook.

"Take him in and turn him over to Ox, George."

Tom stood still. He didn't know what to say, but he knew he had to ask anyway.

"What is it?" Erlo asked.

"I wondered what my pay would be," Tom said hesitantly.

"Twenty-five cents a day. I got ten cents when I started working here," Erlo said gruffly. "But twenty-five is what we pay a boy now, to start with."

Tom didn't know what to say, but Mr. Hook took him by the arm and led him through the door into the mill.

A maze, it looked like to Tom, with all the chutes coming down from the bins in the stories up above, the filled bags in ranks standing on end of the various meals, brans, flours, mixed feeds, and mashes, cracked and whole corn — some lettered in red, some in black, and some with no lettering at all — and the whole place choked with the smell of milled grain. It would take a long time, Tom thought, to learn his way around through all that.

At the far end a man was bagging bran. He worked in a cloud of dust that puffed and thickened around him every time he opened the chute to fill a new bag. Tom had to admire the way he stopped the rush of bran at exactly the right instant with the bag filled out round and solid, then whipped a length of twine off a peg and closed the bag with a double hitch. He swung the bag to one side as easily as if it had been a pillow and stacked it in place. Then he turned as Mr. Hook spoke his name and stepped towards them out of his dust cloud.

"Ox," Mr. Hook said, "this here's Tom Dolan. He's going to work for us."

He was an old man, pretty near as old, Tom thought, as Erlo Ackerman, but a lot bigger, heavy-chested, with a bent-kneed way of walking that was like a bear's. When he put his hand out for Tom to shake, it was like taking hold of the butt end of a ham.

"Pleased to meet you, Tom," he said with a slow smile. And Tom felt more at ease than he had at any time since he had entered the mill.

Mr. Hook broke in to say, "All right, Ox. I'll leave him to you."

He walked back towards the office, and the big man asked, "Ever worked in a feed mill, Tom?"

Tom said he hadn't.

"Well, the main thing is learning what's bagged where and which chute pours which kind of meal. Are them your good clothes?"

Tom said they were.

"Too bad to get them all dust," Ox said. "But I guess they'll shake out. I tell you what. I'll just finish bagging up this lot of bran and then you and me will go all over this mill."

◆ ◆ ◆

That was how Tom Dolan went to work for Ackerman and Hook. The first day, going around with Ox, he found things confusing. It didn't seem he would ever learn which chute let down which meal or grain, and he wondered why they weren't labeled. He was too shy to ask, but then, before he knew it, he found that when Ox told him to pull a sack of laying mash or cracked corn, he went to the right chute instinctively. There was always a small identifying heap on the floor under the chute to check with, and before long he got so he could fill and tie off the bag almost as handy as Ox himself. Of course he didn't have the heft to handle the bag the way Ox could, but he could manage it all right with a hand truck.

Ox made it easy for him. He showed Tom clues to remember things by. When Tom got things wrong, Ox didn't raise his voice. He was slow and patient. Pretty soon Tom learned that his real name was Marvin Hubbard. He had two children, grown up and gone from home, and his wife was poorly. When he wasn't in the mill, he spent his time looking after her.

Perhaps that was why he got to talking more and more with Tom and pretty soon having his lunch with him, when business didn't interfere.

Usually they went out on the loading platform if the weather was fine, sitting on the floor with their backs against the mill wall, shaded by the roof. The other two mill hands usually joined them. They were French-Canadian and brothers, Bancel and Louis Moucheaud, and they were inclined to be excitable, talking in loud voices and arguing with each other, or anybody else for that matter. They could never get Ox into a dispute, though. He only smiled at them and went on with his work, but one day he told Tom that in his opinion, if you translated their name into English, it would probably come out "much odd."

Sometimes their lunch would be interrupted by a customer driving down from the depot with an order. Generally Louis or Bancel would take care of that. Or it would be Mr. Hook coming from the office with an errand for Tom to run. The very first day he told Tom to go up to the pharmacy on Main Street for half a dozen Wheeling Stogies for Erlo Ackerman. But Herman Bondwin, the pharmacist, who didn't know Tom from Adam, was skeptical about a youngster coming to get stogie cigars like that and said Tom would have to have a note signed by Mr. Ackerman if he expected to be given any. Tom went back and told Erlo, and he got uneasy when the old man stared at him with hard and bulging eyes for almost a minute without saying a word. But then he heaved himself out of his chair and said, "All right, Tom. Come along and we'll go and have a little talk with Herman."

Erlo was slow and heavy in his walking but they got up to

Main Street after a while and walked into the pharmacy. Tom could see Mr. Bondwin behind his dispensing counter, but apparently Erlo didn't because he went over to the tobacco counter on the other wall and brought his hand down three or four times on the desk bell standing on it, waiting there with his back to the store till Mr. Bondwin came around to wait on him.

"Yes, Erlo," he said. "Can I do anything for you?"

"You can," Erlo said, his breathing heavy. "You can give Tom Dolan here the six Wheeling Stogie ceegars I asked him to get me half an hour ago. You can charge them to my account, Herman. Or do I still have an account here?"

Mr. Bondwin put on a smile which Tom thought didn't fit his face too well.

"You sure do, Erlo," he said.

"Well, then," Erlo said, "if you'll put them in a twist of paper, and give them to Tom Dolan, here, I'll be obliged."

He waited, his breathing sounding through the store till Mr. Bondwin had done so.

"Herman," he said then, "now you know Tom Dolan works for me. If he works for me, he can be trusted. I knew his grandpa, Chick Hannaberry. I used to go fishing with him. And I knew his ma, Polly Ann, while she was growing up and the prettiest girl on the other side of Black River, and the prettiest on this side too, if it comes to that. And if I send Tom to you for six Wheeling Stogie ceegars that smoke pink and lilac, I want you to let him have them. You understand?"

He put his hand on Tom's shoulder and turned him towards the street door. They went out and they walked back down to the mill, just as slow as they had come up, and Erlo Ackerman didn't say a word more till they got to the office steps.

"You can hand me those stogie ceegars now," he told Tom then and went inside.

It seemed to Tom a strange way to take care of the matter, but just the same he felt good inside.

He felt as if he belonged there at Ackerman and Hook's mill. He had never had the feeling of belonging in a place with grown men before.

◆ ◆ ◆

Tom was late getting home that first evening. The mill didn't close till six-thirty and the three-mile walk back to his own place seemed a lot longer than he had expected it would. But he went up on the kitchen stoop with the good feeling still inside him. Polly Ann came to the door with a kitchen spoon in her hand and her face flushed from the stove. When she saw the white dust all over his good clothes her jaw fell, but she didn't say anything. He could tell by the smell she had made corned beef hash for supper. It smelled fine.

"Hello, Ma," he said. "I'm back. I got the job. It's for one week, though. For trial."

She smiled. "Then you'll keep it, for sure, Tom."

He washed his hands and face at the basin on the porch shelf while she took his jacket and shook what dust she could from it.

"I'll wear my old overalls after this," he said. "But Mr. Ackerman thought I ought to start right in today."

She nodded. "Best not to think about it, Tom."

In the kitchen Cissie-Mae and Ellie were already seated at the table with a coloring book. They wanted to know what Tom had been doing up in town to make him so late, but he didn't tell them much. It was only when he and Polly Ann had the kitchen to themselves that he started to tell her how his day had been. When he got to the part about going up with Erlo Ackerman to see the pharmacist and how Erlo had said she was his mother and he had known her growing up and how pretty she was, Polly Ann turned pink. She said that was just nonsense and Erlo's noddle must be overaged. But Tom could see she liked it.

He told her he would get twenty-five cents a day to start with and she thought it was fair enough.

"They'll pay more in a while," she told him firmly.

After the supper things were cleared away, they went down to the barn to shut the doors, though Drew was the only creature in it — unless a new batch of kittens had arrived. It was dark and when they got back to the kitchen, Tom sat down at the table with a paper block and started to do some figuring.

It seemed to him he ought to put half his pay into Polly Ann's keeping for the family, and at twenty-five cents a day that meant that he could save $39 a year for himself, and most of that could go for buying the Breen barn — if Mrs. Breen was willing to sell.

Then he tried how it would go if he got thirty cents a day. It came all the way to $93.60 a year, out of which he could keep $46.80. At that rate the barn seemed a lot closer in reach. Then he wondered what forty cents a day would do, and by his figuring it gave him $124.80 a year. He stopped right there. He might never get to earn that much money in his whole life. It was too much money even to think about now. He was afraid doing so would make him softheaded. Still, he tore the sheet of paper off the block and took it up to bed with him. He put it in the drawer of the table that served him for a bureau. He didn't have to look at it, only to know that it was there. Next morning, when he got up, he didn't even think about it.

It was quarter to five, because he had to be at the mill at half past seven and before then he had to get the cows and help with milking, eat his breakfast, and walk the three miles to the mill. They would be slower than the miles coming home, being mostly uphill. Later on, when the nights got so cold they would keep the cows in, he would save some time, but then the walking would be harder, especially when there was snow. The town road crew didn't do snow plowing. Each farmer broke road with his sleigh from his place to the next and Tom wouldn't always be able to count on the road being plowed all the way to town.

But the fall stayed open well into December. With early dark, Ackerman's closed earlier, and by that time Tom had got used to his job there. He felt easy with the men. Louis and Bancel Moucheaud every now and then would play a practical joke on him, but that didn't bother him; and Ox said they wouldn't do that kind of thing if they hadn't taken a liking to him. They never tried a joke on Ox. One man had, they said, a young fellow, six feet tall and muscle-proud. He had found Ox on the second floor of the mill and taken a measure of bran out of a hopper and poured it over Ox's head. They said it took a minute for Ox to clean his eyeglasses and get his eyes free of the bran. But then with a sudden move he had come up behind the smart aleck and taken him by the collar of his shirt and the seat of his pants and swung him up over his head. Louis and Bancel said that Ox carried the big squirt that way back to the bran hopper and with kind of a flip tossed him head first into it. It took the squirt quite a while to get himself upright in the bin and scramble out. He had nothing to say, either, to Ox; but he took his trade to Bisbee's feedstore on Main Street after that. Neither Erlo nor George Hook seemed to mind, though, when they heard the story.

The customers coming in from farms all over the township, and even from the neighboring ones over the county line, generally passed more or less time talking with the mill people, sometimes about the feed they were buying and more often about what was going on on neighbor farms as well as their own. In this way Tom now and then heard about the Widow Breen.

People wondered how she could go on living way off there all by herself. She didn't do anything except not die, they said. Some of their women thought it was cruel awful for a body to be left that way. But Joe Hemphill from the livery, who fetched her into town once a month to trade for groceries and such, said that was how she liked it. She was real chirpy for so old a body, he said, and talked quite a lot on their rides into town and back, but she wasn't interested a bit in what became of other people. She talked about the wild animals that came around her place or her cat, Tabs; only she was getting kind of worried about him now, him being so old.

Tom always tried to get to fill Joe Hemphill's order so he could listen to him talk about the Widow Breen. He wanted to ask how her barn was holding up, but he didn't want other people knowing he was interested in it. And every day something else turned up in the talk at the mill to run his mind from the old woman, at least until Joe Hemphill came again with his spring wagon for oats and mash for the livery horses.

The days spun out and kept getting shorter as December turned towards Christmas. His walk home now was in the dark and it was getting a lot colder. One night after eating, he looked in the box he kept his savings in and found he had thirteen dollars and a quarter saved. It was more money than he had ever had of his own. More than he had ever seen in Polly Ann's possession, at least that didn't have to be spent next day for groceries or to pay off something she owed on. It kept him awake for close to half an hour, wondering whether he should take some of it out and maybe buy some Christmas gifts for Polly Ann and his sisters.

He had no idea how much that would be, but just before dropping off to sleep he thought two dollars and a quarter might do it. It seemed a lot, but he had never had money to buy presents with before and he figured he could afford it. Next morning, though, it seemed an awful big fraction of his total savings. He tried putting a dollar back in the box, but a dollar and a quarter hardly seemed enough. Then he put the quarter back, but somehow it seemed better to leave the round sum of eleven dollars. Even so he didn't know whether the two dollars and a quarter would be enough to take care of the girls as well as Polly Ann. In the end he put the two dollars and a quarter in his pocket the way he'd planned and came downstairs.

It was biting cold when he went to the barn and still pitch-dark. His breath fogged against the light when he hung the lantern over the run between the cows. He had begun milking when Polly Ann came in, her cheeks bright from the cold, and he saw suddenly that she was a pretty woman, as Erlo Ackerman had remembered her being as a girl. Right then he knew that taking out the full two dollars and a quarter had been the right thing to do. He didn't know what he would find to get her. Something to wear, most likely; something pretty.

Thinking what he might buy for her helped to shorten his long walk, but as he came up the steep pitch to the canal bridge, it started to snow, a few scattered flakes whirling on the beginning of a northeast wind, and a long way before he reached the mill the cold had eaten in through his clothes. Ox took one look at him and hustled him right into the office where a big fire roared in the stove. Mr. Hook was there, sitting with his boots against the stove rail, but Erlo Ackerman hadn't showed up yet.

He came in, though, a minute later, pausing inside the door to knock the snow from his hat and shake out his overcoat.

Ox said, "I brought Tom in here to get warmed up."

Erlo nodded. "It's a long walk," he said. "And it looks to me it's going to get worse. Like winter's really got here now."

It seemed he must be right. The snow mounted up all morning and not many customers turned up. Bancel said you had to expect it. Beginning snow made it a time between rolling and sliding; there wasn't yet enough snow for a pung and a farmer didn't like to come with his lumber wagon for fear the snow would get too deep. They hung around in the mill with the doors closed onto the loading platform, occasionally going into the office to warm up, and towards noon Tom asked Ox if he could go up to Main Street in his lunch hour to do his Christmas shopping.

"Why, yes," Ox said. "I'd forgot it's only three days to Christmas. I better do my own, but you get along now. We won't need you here the way things are going."

◆ ◆ ◆

There were three inches of snow on the sidewalk. The elm trees on the village green, which was shaped like a triangle, were white with it and the bandstand underneath them looked like a cake, sugar-frosted. He walked down Main Street under the storekeepers' signs looking for Baker's Millinery. It was the first time he had ever walked along the storefronts with money to spend in his pocket, and he felt a bit strange and self-conscious. But he made up his mind he wouldn't let that stop him from going straight into the store.

Only it didn't work out that way. When he got to the store window there was a sheet that looked as if it had come out of a newspaper stuck to the inside of the glass. It said, SPECIAL PRE-CHRISTMAS OFFERINGS. There was a series of money figures and underneath the goods offered at that figure. The first was 10¢, but it didn't include anything that looked suitable for Polly Ann. The next one was 17¢. He couldn't find anything there, either, though it did list Hair ribbons, Silk, that might do for Cissie-Mae and Ellie. He stayed there, reading down the list with the snow thickening on his cap and shoulders, through 75¢, where it said, *Here are goods worth $1.00 to $1.25, and the buyer saves the price of a dinner,* which Tom thought a tempting offer except there was nothing in it he fancied for Polly Ann.

The next group was headed $1.00: *Items good enough for a Queen; cheap enough at $2.00,* which raised his hopes, but it seemed to include nothing but ladies' underwear, and he didn't think that was quite the thing a boy ought to buy for his mother.

So it came down to the final category, listed at $2.00-$2.50, and underneath it said, *Choicest Millinery Offerings this side of New York City. Even in the Great Metropolis you will not find Many Items duplicating These.* It surely did sound interesting, and then Tom spotted in the listed items Ladies' Fine Shirtwaists; and it seemed as if that might be just the thing to give to Polly Ann. A new shirtwaist, which she could put right on for Christmas Day itself. He drew a deep breath and with his hand clutching the money in his pants pocket walked into the store.

Inside the store there were a lot of counters, with salesladies behind some of them and a lot of female customers looking over the goods. They all seemed to be talking to each other, their voices high-pitched and excited, kind of like chicken voices in a yard, when one hen or another had scratched up something special. Tom felt a kind of wildness in his eye as he looked around. There wasn't another man or boy in the whole enduring store. It would have been easier if he had had any idea where they had the shirtwaists laid out, but he didn't, and all of a sudden he found that he was plain scared of asking.

But then a saleslady turned up beside him and asked if she could help him in any way, and he gulped and said maybe she could. But then his voice drew abruptly to a close, so she had to ask was there anything special he was looking for? And he said he was looking for a present to give someone at Christmas.

She asked, did he have any idea what kind of thing?

And he said, his voice back where it ought to be, a shirtwaist, maybe. So she took him over to a counter on the far side and asked if he had any particular sort in mind.

"It has got to be one of the two-dollar ones," he told her, looking up at her for the first time. To his surprise she was quite young, maybe younger than his mother herself.

"Well," she said, "we have some real nice ones. Do you know the size?"

That was something Tom hadn't even thought about, and he got to feeling desperate. The saleslady saw from the way he looked that he didn't have the remotest idea.

"Maybe we can figure it out," she said. "How tall is your friend compared to you?"

"It's for my mother," he blurted. "And she's small, not much over the top of my shoulder. I mean the top of her head's not much more than that."

"I see," the saleslady said. "Is she stout-built?"

"Oh no!" he exclaimed. "She's made real small."

"I see," the saleslady said again. "I should think that might be a thirty-four. You don't see too many ladies that size around here. I wonder if I might know her."

"She's Polly Ann Dolan," Tom told her.

She smiled. What seemed to him a very nice smile.

"Why, I know who she is," she said, "and I'm sure a thirty-two would be just right."

She reached into the counter and brought out several shirtwaists of that size and laid them out on top for Tom to take his pick. It took him a while. Costing two dollars, he wanted to make sure it would be one that suited Polly Ann's looks. In the end he picked one with a bit of ruffling around the neck and down the front where it buttoned.

The saleslady seemed to approve.

"I'm sure she's going to like it," she said.

He was mightily relieved, but he had another anxious moment when she took his money and the shirtwaist somewhere to the back of the store. However, in a few minutes she was back, handing him a done-up package, and the strange thing to him was that she said thank you after taking so much pains to help him. So he thanked her, which seemed more reasonable, and got out of the store as quickly as he could.

The snow was still coming down, heavier than before, and standing on the sidewalk, his hat all whitened with it, was Mr. Hook. He looked surprised to see Tom coming out of Baker's Millinery.

"Christmas shopping, Tom?"

Tom allowed he was. And then suddenly remembered that he hadn't got the hair ribbons he'd been thinking of for Cissie-Mae and Ellie. He grinned a little sheepishly at Mr. Hook, admitting he'd forgotten part of his errand.

"Well, go back in," Mr. Hook told him. "If you're quick we can walk back down to the mill together."

So Tom ducked back through the door. It was easier this second time and besides, he had seen where the hair ribbons were displayed and could go right over to them. A saleslady was standing there. She was older than the first one and got the transaction over in jig time. He bought a blue one for Ellie and a red one for Cissie-Mae, and paid her the quarter. When she came back with the ribbons in a package, she gave him his change, which meant that he had eight cents left over from his Christmas buying. More than he had expected.

The Wonderful Mirror

Charles J. Finger

This is the tale of Suso who was the daughter of a very rich man, a very kind-hearted one, too. Never was beggar turned from his door, nor in the length and breadth of his land was there hunger or want. And he loved Suso no less than she loved him. She was very close to his heart and all that could be done to make her happy he did. As for her, there was no pleasure in her day if she was not assured of his happiness.

When her sister had left home to be married, Suso and her father had gone about planning a great park which Suso was to have for her own, a park of terraced, flowered hills. And when it was finished, both birds and animals came to live there and the air was full of song. So in that place Suso played with her companions, and their hearts were in tune with the beauty all about. It was a never-ending pleasure to seek out new places in the great park, cool nooks in which were little waterfalls whose silver music mingled with the whispering of the leaves, or shaded spots where were ponds of crystal water and fountains and seats and bright green carpets of moss.

For a long time there was happiness, until, indeed, her

father married again, for her mother had died when Suso was a small child. Then one day there was a cloud of grief in the maiden's heart, because on a silent, moonlit night she had walked with her father and he had told her that he was troubled with a wasting sickness and feared that he had not long to live. Some enemy, he said, had cast a spell on him, so that day by day he grew weaker and weaker and weaker. Wise men and doctors had looked into the matter, had sat solemnly and thought, had guessed and wondered, but had agreed on one thing only — that something was wrong. What that something was they did not know, but they agreed that if the thing that was wrong could be discovered and removed, all would go well again. Because of what her father had told her, Suso was sad and often wandered to a quiet place where she could tell her troubles to the trees.

The stepmother was not at all fair in her ways and not only disliked Suso, but was very mean and treacherous, hiding her hatred from the father and petting Suso when he was near, stroking her hair and saying pretty things. So well did the wicked woman play her part that nothing could have made the father believe other than that she loved Suso quite as much as he did. For instance, on that moonlit night when he had told his daughter of his trouble, seeing her tears, for she had wept bitterly, he had said:

"But Suso, my dove, your mother will care for you tenderly when I am dead, for she loves you dearly."

At that the girl stifled her sobs and dried her tears, lest the father she loved so well should be wounded by her grief, and seeing her calmed he had supposed that all was well and that his words had soothed her.

But see how it really was with Suso and her stepmother. There was one day, not long after, when father and stepmother and daughter were standing by the fountain, watching the wavering shadows flying across the green, when the man suddenly felt a clutching pain at his heart and was forced to sit down for very weakness. When he felt a little better and the first sharpness of the pain had gone, Suso walked with him to the house, and when he was comfortably seated and had a feather robe cast about him, he bade her return to her stepmother. That she did, because she was bid, although her wish would have been to sit at his feet. Because of her unwillingness and her grief she went softly, and not singing and dancing, as was her fashion. And what was her terror when she saw and heard the wicked woman talking to a great horned owl that sat in the hollow of an old tree! So terrible that seemed, that Suso could find nothing to say, but stood with clasped hands, her heart a-flutter. Seeing Suso, the woman motioned to the owl and the bird said no more, but sat listening, its head on one side. Then the stepmother took Suso by the hand and drew her into a place where they could be seen by the father, but far enough away to be out of earshot. But the father, seeing the woman and the maiden standing thus together, was happy, thinking that his daughter had a friend. It made him happier still to see the woman take Suso's arm and pull it gently about her waist. But he did not hear what was said, for had he heard, it would have cut him to the heart.

This is what the woman said, and her voice was like a poison-dart as she whispered loud enough for the owl to hear:

"Suso, stand thus with your arm about my waist so that your father may see us together. Thus he will think that I love you." Then she hissed in the girl's ear: "But I hate you, hate you, hate you."

And the owl lifted his head, blew a little and repeated softly: "Hate you — Hoo! — Hoo!"

From far off in the woods came the sound of an answering owl like an echo: "Hate you — Hoo! — Hoo!" and it seemed to Suso that all the world hated her for no cause, for the screeching parrots, too, repeated the cry. As for the sweet feathered things that she loved, they had all fled from that place.

Soon the stepmother spoke again and the owl dropped to a lower branch the better to hear. "Suso," said the woman, "your father cannot live much longer. The spell is upon him and day by day he nears his death. Because of that I am glad, for when he dies, all this land, the house, and all its riches, must be mine."

Hearing that vicious speech Suso was well nigh faint with fear and horror and would have sped to her father to warn him. But the woman caught her by the wrist, twisting it painfully, and pinched the soft place on her arm with her other hand, and stooping again so that it seemed to the watching father that she kissed Suso, she said:

"But see to it that you say no word, for the moment that you say anything but good of me, that moment your father will fall dead."

So what was Suso to do?

Thus it was that Suso crept to quiet places and told her tale to the whispering leaves and to the evening breeze, and thus it was that in the midst of all that beauty of golden sunlight and silver-glinted waters and flower-twined forest she could not but be sad. For there were tears in her heart, and everything that her father did for her was as nothing and like a crumbling tower.

But she had told the trees (and trees bend their tops though they are foot-fast, and leaves, too, whisper one to another), so that the tale went abroad, though of this, Suso knew nothing.

Now while all this was going on there lived in the hills far off a youth, and his name was Huathia. Brown-haired he was and bright-eyed too, with clear skin and strong arms, and all who knew him said that he was a good lad and honest.

He was a herder of goats and llamas, and one day, as he was out in the *vega* with his flock, he chanced to see a falcon wheeling high in the air, carrying something in its beak that sent the rays of the sun flashing far, like silver light. Then the bird dipped with the thing it was carrying, looking like a glittering falling star, and Huathia for a moment lost sight of the bird as it dropped behind a bush. But it soon rose and took to flight, this time without the shining thing. So Huathia went to the place where the falcon had dropped, and there at the bottom of a little stream he saw a bright round piece of silver. The lad rescued it and looked at it with astonishment as it lay in his hand, a polished and smooth disc it was, that reflected his face as clearly as a mirror. So he kept it, wrapping it in a leaf, and took it that night to the place where the lad lived with another herdsman, a very wise and good man who knew many strange things, and he told the youth that it was the wonderful mirror of one called Paracaca, long since dead. He said that whoever looked in it saw his own face as others saw it, but the owner of the mirror saw something else, "for," added he, "with it you may see the hidden spirit of other people, seeing through the mask they wear. And if a man has the face of a man but the heart of a fox then certainly while such a man beholds his own face, you shall see the other creature in him."

Hearing that, the youth Huathia was much amazed at the magic of the thing and, holding it so that the face of his herder friend was shown in the mirror, saw, not the rough bearded face of the man alone, all knotted like a tree-trunk, but a face that was full of kindness and gentleness, at which he was glad.

So he placed the wonderful mirror in his bag and carried it about with him. The next day, while he was leaning against the trunk of a tree and playing on his flute, he seemed to hear a whispering, and putting his reed away he listened intently. Still and small, still and small were the voices that he heard, as tree-head bent to tree-head and leaf murmured to leaf, but soon he caught the rumour that ran, and learned the tale that in the country of the rich man there was a creature timorous and frail, whose gentle heart was heavy with sorrow, and that an unknown evil brooded dark.

No time lost he then, seeing that there was something of worth that he could possibly do, but gave the care of the goats and llamas to his friend, took his arrows and bow, his bag with a little food and the wonderful mirror, and after bidding his friend good-bye set off for the land of the rich man. What was strange was that while all had been silent in the soft green woods that morning, except for the sound of his flute, no sooner had he started on his way than a gay chorus came from the bright birds and the world was full of mirth. So, well content, he went on his way, a ragged herdsman, but light of heart and strong of limb and brave.

Into the land of the rich man he went and came in time to a place where sat the maiden under a tree, doves at her feet and glittering humming-birds about her head. When Suso saw the youth her heart leaped for joy, for she knew him for a kind lad, though never before had she set eyes on him.

"Are you a beggar and poor?" she asked. "For here there is plenty for all."

"I am no beggar," he answered, "and for myself I am well content with what I have. But it has been whispered about the world and I have heard the tale, that there is a great sorrow upon you, and that some unknown evil is destroying the beauty and the bliss of this place, so I have come to do what is to be done."

At that Suso said no more but rose up and took Huathia by the hand and led him to her father. It was a day on which the good man was very weak, but seeing that his daughter was pleased with her new companion he ordered his servants to spread a table under the trees, and the three of them had a feast of goat's milk and fruit, and cassava bread, though the father could eat but little. Then Huathia took his flute and played sweet music until the world seemed full of peace, and gripping grief had vanished. Suso, too, sang sweetly, so that for a moment the father thought that the shadow that was upon him was but a dream and might pass.

They talked long and long, the three of them, and Huathia learned much about the rich man's failing strength, whereupon it came to him somehow, that by means of his wonderful mirror he might perchance discover what evil thing was about that place. To him the rich man said:

"If with this mirror you can find the hidden evil thing and

can restore my strength again, then there is nothing too great that I own which may not be yours for the asking."

"There is but one thing I want," said Huathia. "For I love Suso the gentle and would marry her."

The rich man thought long after this speech, stroking the hair of Suso who sat at his knee, for it had not entered into his mind that his daughter might be the gift which the youth demanded as his price. But looking at the maiden he saw that her eyes were cast down, though for a moment they had looked up swiftly as Huathia spoke. Then, too, it was certain that since the youth had been there, the song of the birds was louder in the thicket and the green of the trees brighter.

So the father said thoughtfully: "If you find the cause of the trouble that is upon me and relieve it so that I am healed again, then you may have my daughter for your wife, though you must promise me that you will stay in this place."

That, Huathia promised readily enough, and stooped to Suso and kissed her, and having done so, went away to the dark pool in the woods to sleep, at the very moment the stepmother came out of the house to join her husband and his daughter.

As it happened that night, there was a thin new moon, and the youth slept but little because of the croaking noise made by the frogs. Presently, full awake, he sat up, and it seemed to him that the air was full of noise, not only of frogs but of the hooting of owls and the whirring of bats, and looking he saw the strange sight of a great white toad with two heads, and presently about that fearful thing other things gathered. From rock and hole came unclean creatures, abominable serpents and centipedes and great gray spiders, and all these gathered in a circle, the two-headed toad in the centre. With wide-open eyes Huathia watched, although the sight of so much that was noisome came near to benumbing and stupefying him, and incomplete shapes seemed to be looking at him with evil eyes from the black depth of the forest.

Soon the owl began to mourn and the song fell into words and the youth heard this:

"Who knows where hides our queen? Hoo! Hoo!"

And first one creature and then another answered:

"The toad, our queen, lies hid unsought
Beneath the stone that men have wrought."

And so it went on, a mad and horrible concert, with bat and owl and great ghost-moth whirling about on silent wings, until sickened of it all Huathia rose up and clapping his hands to his ears fled from the place. And when he had gained a quiet and lonely spot he sat down, but in his ears rang what he had heard:

"The toad, our queen, lies hid unsought
Beneath the stone that men have wrought."

So he wondered and wondered where could be the stone that men had wrought, and the story that men had told of a great temple on the mountains came to him. But that place seemed too far away.

When it was full day the youth went to the house, and in time the rich man came forth and greeted him. Then came the stepmother, who fixed her large dark eyes on Huathia, not looking at him straight, but sideways. Suso came shortly afterward and the youth could not take his eyes from her. It seemed to him that she was the most beautiful of living things as she sat on her stool by the side of her father, her hair touched by the golden light so that it seemed to be as full of ripples as a sun-kissed brook. So there was pleasant talk while they ate, and, after, a drinking-in of soft music as Huathia played on his flute. Suso sang when Huathia had finished, and though her song had a touch of sadness in it, it seemed to her pleased father that all on earth that was soft and shapely and fair was gathered there in that garden, until catching the eye of his wife he was reminded that his life was flowing away, and the old grief came upon him.

Somehow talk fell upon Huathia and his mirror and the strange way in which he had found it, and he took it from his bag. As he looked in it, Suso came and stood behind him, so that he saw the reflection of her face and the true picture of herself, and there was a gentleness there, the gentleness of the dove and the purity of the flower. The rich man came, too, looking over Huathia's shoulder and saw his own reflection. But what the youth saw was a face that denoted great bravery and kindness. Seeing all this the stepmother stretched her hand across the table and took the mirror, gazing at the picture of her own dark beauty. Then Huathia stepped to her side and looked into the disc. He saw, not the dark eyes and night-black hair that she saw, not the face of a proud woman, but the face of a toad, and when she held the polished silver further off, the better to see, the toad-face changed, so that he saw a double-headed toad. But of that she knew nothing and did not even guess that he knew her for a vile witch and no true woman. And as she continued to gaze and her thoughts wandered, so did new things come into the picture that Huathia saw, and he beheld about her neck two writhing white snakes, a sight so horrible that he could scarcely hold his countenance or prevent himself from calling out. Having seen to her content, the woman rose from her stool and left the room.

The rich man, already tired, for his night's sleep did not revive him, stood up and beckoned to the youth to give him an arm. Suso supported him on the other side and so they walked slowly to a seat beneath a great flowering bush near the house. Having found his seat and being wrapped in his feather mantle by Suso, he asked the youth to play the flute again. Huathia was ready and willing, but somehow the memory of the two-headed toad and the two white snakes made him nervous, and when he put his flute to his lips no sweet sounds came, but instead rude noises like the hissing of snakes and the croaking of frogs and the screeching of parrots. Even Suso stopped her ears and her father bade the youth cease his noise.

"Are you of those who make my last days the wearier with your noises?" he said sorrowfully. Then he added: "For many nights I have dreamed of toads with two heads and of snakes that hung over me, and now you come with your flute and the noises that such evil things make. I had expected better of you, Huathia, seeing that I have treated you as a son."

Huathia earnestly assured him that he had no wish to do other than to make music, and he ended by saying: "There is, I am sure, some enchantment in this place, for though the sun is warm I feel a chill, as if some clammy thing enfolded me."

He shivered as he spoke, though he was a lad whose blood

ran warm; not afraid, not given to idle fancies. Of a sudden his eyes fell upon a large grindstone that lay nearby. It was a stone so great that two men could hardly make shift to raise it, and so it had been left there for years and grasses had grown about it. But when Huathia saw it, there leaped into his mind the song that he had heard:

"The toad, our queen, lies hid unsought
Beneath the stone that men have wrought."

It had meant little in the night, but in a flash he saw that the grindstone was a stone wrought by men. So fitting an arrow to his bow he handed the weapon to Suso, telling her to shoot whatever evil thing was discovered when he lifted the stone. With a great effort he raised the stone suddenly, heavy though it was, lifting it high above his head, and there, in a hollow place where the stone had been, sat a large, white, double-headed toad.

"Shoot, Suso, shoot!" commanded the father. "Let not that evil thing escape. It is the creature that torments me at night."

Swift flew the arrow and it pierced the body of the toad. At the same moment there fell from the roof of the house two monstrous white serpents where they had lain hidden. Like lightning Huathia, having seized the bow, sent two arrows flying, and each serpent was cut into halves. In less than three moments three evil things died, and it was like the sun coming from a cloud-veil, the way in which joy came to that place. The weakness of the father fell from him like a cloak. The bodies of the toad and the snakes withered and shriveled, and as a light breeze sprang up, what was left of them was blown away as dust. There were soft stirrings in the thicket and the whole world burst into song. So both father and daughter knew then that the witcheries were gone and the evil creatures vanished forever, and that all the trouble that had been upon that place came from the wicked stepmother.

So youth and maiden were married, and the father soon regained his health and strength, and in all the world there were no happier people than they.

Aunt Charity Arrives in New England

Lois Lenski

"A sail! A sail!" The cry came from a dark-skinned, half-grown boy, who flew fleet as the wind, past the open door. His long arm, upraised, pointed toward the open sea.

Goodwife Partridge and her children hastened out.

"Today it comes!" announced Seaborn, the eldest boy, solemnly.

"Who was it? What said he?" cried the Goodwife.

" 'Twas Know-God, the Indian boy," explained Seaborn. "The long-awaited ship from England cometh at last."

"Know-God hath seen a sail!" piped up little Waitstill.

Goodwife Partridge held God-be-thanked, the babe, on one arm. She lifted her hand to shade her eyes.

The late October sun shone softly upon the group before the low, straw-thatched cottage. It bathed in mellow warmth the fort on the hill as well as the houses that lined the winding path and clustered at the water's edge. It traced in shining light the course of the river making its way to the blue sea beyond.

"I see naught!" cried Goodwife Partridge, in vexation. "A few fishing shallops near shore and naught else."

"But Know-God's eyes be black as jet!" cried Waitstill, in excitement. "Black eyes be strongest for sight. Pale blue eyes like ours cannot see half so well."

"But the Crier — hath he cried the ship?" asked Goodwife Partridge. "See you the Crier, childer? Hear you his bell?"

"Oh, Ma'am, will Aunt Charity come?" asked eight-year-old Comfort.

"Will the ship bring her?" echoed Thankful, her sister, but one year younger.

The two girls might have been twins, except that one was shorter than the other. Like their mother, they were dressed in Puritan costume, long full petticoats and tight-fitting waistcoats of russet-colored cloth, relieved by calico aprons and falling collars. White lawn coifs or caps fitted close to their shapely heads.

"Know-God's eyes be, indeed, far-seeing," said Seaborn sternly. "Parson Humphrey saith he hath the intelligence of the Devil. He hath oft told of a ship at sea, which he hath seen sooner by one hour, yea two hours, than any English man that stood by of purpose to look out."

The little group stood silent, their eyes strained toward the brightness of the sea. Behind them a crude fence of split palings enclosed a tiny yard where, on both sides of the trim clam-shell path, grew a few straggling vegetables and herbs.

A stir of activity began along shore. Men and boys appeared on the wharves which had been empty before. Running figures moved swiftly along the descending paths.

People looked out of doors and windows. The seaport came to life.

"Look ye! The sail! I see it plain!" cried Waitstill.

A white speck could now be seen against the blue. Soon it was in the bay, growing larger and whiter each moment. Then the clang of a bell rang out.

"Good news! Good news!" came the Town Crier's shout. "A ship from England . . . a ship from England docks this day!"

Up the grassy path strode the stooped and bent figure of a man, bell in hand. His voice was harsh, his bell-clang harsher, and his face belied the welcome of his news. Sour and cross he looked, as if he grudged the bringing of cheer and hated all happiness.

"Go ye, find your father, lads," said Goodwife Partridge quickly. "He works with the thatchers in the marsh grasses along the beach. Tell him the news — a ship cometh. He will do well to fetch home fresh fish or game for supper."

The two boys hurried off.

"Will then our Aunt Charity come?" asked Comfort again.

But Goodwife Partridge's heart was too full for answer. Food and clothing, letters and news of dear ones — a ship from home meant all these things. But this time more, perhaps. Perhaps sister Charity *would* be aboard. Little Charity, left behind a mere child in England, ten years before. Now a woman grown, a woman young in years, but old enough to have borne the sorrow of loss of both their parents and of her newly married husband.

It was now a year since Goodwife Partridge had had Parson Humphrey write the letter which bade her come out to her sister in the new world. There had been no reply. Each ship brought the hope that Charity might come, but she had not. A new ship meant new hope. Would Charity come and would her sister know her if she came?

Goodwife Partridge made haste to the kitchen to stir up an extra batch of Indian bannock and set it on a board before the open fire. With the birch-twig broom, Thankful hastily swept stray ashes from the great stone hearth. Comfort ran, at her mother's bidding, and brought a piggin of water brimful from the spring hard by the kitchen door.

Goodwife Partridge grasped the ladle and stirred briskly the pumpkin sauce which simmered and bubbled in the great iron pot.

"I fear 'twill burn, with no one to mind it," she said.

"I will bide at home, Ma'am," said Thankful, "and stir the pumpkin sauce."

"Ay, 'tis well, daughter. Bide ye here. Comfort goes with me to mind the babe."

The wharf was packed when the good ship *Fearless* dropped anchor alongside. A brave sight she was, with her great cabin, lofty poop, fighting tops, lateen-rigged mizzen, whipstaff and high forecastle. But the thin-faced passengers looked worn and weary as, with outstretched arms and glad cries, they leaned far out over the rail. The waves slapped against the gunwale, the sailors tugged at the ropes, and while seagulls cried mournfully overhead, the passengers stepped ashore.

"Charity hath bonny blue eyes and brown hair that curls. Her cheeks were ever ruddy — I see her yet. Always merry, always skipping and running she was. We called each other 'Madcap' and 'Mischief' for pet names. Sometimes graver people called her a *hoyting* girl, but she meant no one harm . . ."

Her mother spoke as if to herself, but Comfort listened happily. Of this unknown aunt she never tired hearing.

The townspeople fell back as the newcomers appeared. A woman with three children was noisily welcomed by the Hatherly family. A group of tradesmen, loaded down with tools, were met by the town authorities. An old man, a young couple with a boy at their side, a gentleman and his lady before whom the others stepped aside — these were the newcomers. A babble of greetings, tears and sobs of recognition and welcome, laughter of relief and fear filled the air.

Loud words were bandied back and forth:

"How good to leave the evil-smelling ship and taste the air!"

"A cup of New England's air be better than a whole draught of Old England's ale!"

"The air be sweet! The smell of land be sweet!"

"If this land be not rich, then is the whole world poor."

"Have ye no houses built for us? Where then can we live?"

"No place for those of a dronish disposition . . ."

"So many godly persons were going . . ."

"Our hands be coarse. Here there is work to do."

"God hath brought us safe to land . . ."

"From a paradise of plenty into a wilderness of wants."

"What sound greets my ear? The cry of wild animals in the forest? Ye have lions here that roar?"

"It is a country rather to affright, than to delight one."

"God hath preserved us through our afflictions . . ."

"Have ye no town? No town houses? Only crude hovels at the door of the forest? Ye call this a thriving settlement?"

Comfort Partridge held tight to her small brother's hand, as the words smote her ears.

The seamen hastened out, bringing their goods on shore.

"She hath not come," said Goodwife Partridge sadly. "Wait ye here. I needs must buy lace and hooks and eyes if the seamen's price be not too dear."

She went to the corner of the warehouse where hasty counters of planks had been set up and villagers and seamen began noisily bickering.

Comfort waited with a sinking heart. She wanted Aunt Charity to come. Somehow she knew that Aunt Charity would be different from anyone she had known before. Although she had never seen her, she knew she would greatly love her. But Aunt Charity had not come. A tear stole down her cheek.

"The wind blew mightily, the sea roared, the waves tossed us horribly, but God in his mercy saved us. Scores of cattle were so tossed and bruised they straighatway died." It was the Captain of the *Fearless* speaking.

"How many brought ye?" asked the Magistrate.

"With a brave hundred we started out," growled Captain Boswell. "But three months' battling with storms killed scores, I say."

"What provision brought ye?" The Magistrate's voice was stern.

"When the storms raged, we had to empty great supply of provision and extra store overboard, I tell ye!"

"Overboard!" echoed the Magistrate. "How then shall we feed these people?"

Townsmen crowded close and a general hubbub arose.

Comfort watched the scrawny cattle being dragged off the ship by scolding cowkeepers.

"What mechanics brought ye?" demanded the Magistrate. "We be in sore need of an ingenious carpenter and a cunning joiner. Have ye brought out a good brickmaker, a leather dresser, a handy cooper and a weaver to weave fine cloth? These we have sent for repeatedly."

"Some died on the voyage — 'twas the brickmaker, methinks," replied Captain Boswell, scratching his head. "Or, was it the weaver? There they be yonder," he pointed. "Go ask 'em which died."

The Magistrate turned to the mechanics, but the Captain called him back. "Have ye then good store of salt fish ready? Clapboard and beaver hides for my voyage back to Old England?" But he got no answer.

Little God-be-thanked began to whimper. Comfort took him in her arms. Once more Aunt Charity had not come. The disappointment was hard to bear.

A sudden commotion arose.

"Ye sneak! Ye naughty baggage! I catched ye!"

A seaman appeared, dragging a half-grown, unkempt girl by the arm. Fighting like a tiger, the girl turned and bit the man's arm. He dropped her wrist like a hot coal. Then he cornered her between a pile of barrels and the building.

"Ye won't get away scot-free, no ye won't! Hey, Cap'n Boswell, look ye here at this wench. She's a tryin' to skip without so much as a by-your-leave!"

The Captain and the Magistrate hurried over. The Constable appeared and several tithing-men. Comfort came closer, holding the babe tightly in her arms.

The girl wore no coif or neck-cloth. Her hair fell over her eyes, as her head hung forward with a hang-dog air. She carried a kerchief-tied bundle of clothing. Her petticoat and apron were soiled and torn. She must be a very wicked person, to appear so distraught.

"Hold her fast!" snorted Captain Boswell, in a low voice. "She hath made life miserable for every passenger on board — she hath stolen bisket-cake by the barrel, she hath thieved seven precious lemons and eat them all at one sitting. She hath proved herself a devil of a nuisance." Aloud he shouted: "Here's a husky, fourteen-year-old female, a bargain for anyone who needs a strong-armed servant gal! Who will pay passage for this likely redemptioner?"

The crowd closed in and Comfort was pushed aside. "She hath a sinful heart. How wicked she must be. Who would want a wicked servant?" said Comfort to herself.

Then she saw a fair lady talking to the Captain. Above the crowd she saw the lady's black beaver hat. Below, she caught a glimpse of her gown of fresh flaming silk. Would so fine a lady pay passage for so wicked a servant?

She saw Gaffer and Goodwife Lumpkin hasten up and melt into the crowd. Goody Lumpkin had an unsavory reputation. Her tongue was as sharp as a scissors blade and she never gave it rest. Poor Gaffer Lumpkin led a sorry life and a silent one. They had no children, so Goody Lumpkin longed for a servant. Well, if she bought this one, she might have her hands pretty full. Comfort turned to go.

Then she heard the lady speaking.

"She is but a child. If treated fairly, the best side of her nature can be brought out."

The lady's words were clear and sweet. Her face, turned toward Comfort for a moment, made the child's heart skip a beat. The glance reminded her of something warm and sweet and familiar, she knew not what.

"Evil we punish here in New England," answered the Magistrate.

"She hath had enough of brutality in her short life," retorted the lady. "Why not try kindness? It might save her soul!"

The Magistrate looked the lady up and down. He frowned at her costly apparel. The very color of her shining gown seemed to hurt his eyes.

"Kindness!" he exclaimed. "Punish wrong-doing with kindness!" He jerked the cringing girl to her feet. "Captain Boswell," he shouted, "why brought ye here this wench? We have no place for corrupt and naughty persons in our fair town. Back to England she must go!"

"Never!" replied the Captain. "Some godly woman can make of her a useful servant maid."

"Mistress, wilt buy her yourself?" The Magistrate turned to the lady.

Before she could reply, the two Lumpkins rushed forward.

"No, no, buy her not!" screamed Goody Lumpkin, in haste. Then in a politer tone she added: "Oh, good sir, 'tis *we* who want her." With her sharp elbow she poked her husband in the ribs. "Say what I telled ye to say."

"We take her home . . . my wife, she needeth a goodly serving maid," piped up Gaffer Lumpkin obediently. "I pay her passage money, if she serve us for five years and I give her a she-goat to help her start out in life."

"No, no, no, no!" screamed the girl. She broke away and with outstretched arms, fell imploring at the lady's feet. "Don't let them take me, Ma'am! Don't!"

The lady leaned over and spoke to the girl, whereupon she rose quietly to her feet. Captain Boswell and the Lumpkins talked together and soon the Lumpkins went away with the redemptioner held tightly between them. She tossed her hair aside and looked back once at the lady in the silken gown. Now hath Goody Lumpkin a servant to her liking, thought Comfort.

The Magistrate again looked the lady up and down.

"No place here for those of a dronish disposition, who come in the hope to live in plenty and idleness. No place here for those that would live off the sweat of another man's brows." The words were as harsh and biting as a wintry wind out of the north. "All must be workers in some kind."

The lovely lady bowed her head a trifle. "So I have heard."

"Why then come ye here?" The Magistrate's question was blunt.

"I am a widow, good sir." The lady lifted her chin. "My husband dying so soon after the death of my father and mother . . . my sister sent for me to come out . . ." Her voice trembled and her eyes looked uncertainly about.

"It is the duty of widows and spinsters to serve the whole settlement; to show mercy with cheerfulness and to minister to the sick and poor brethren. See ye to it." The Magistrate started to go but turned back. "Your name then, Mistress?"

"Widow Cummings, sir," replied the lady. "My sister . . ."

Comfort saw her mother coming. Goodwife Partridge, unable to buy the needed articles, hurried back.

"God-be-thanked hath been well-behaved, Ma'am," reported Comfort. "He hath not cried once."

But her mother looked not at her babe, nor did she listen. She saw only the lady standing so still beside the Magistrate. The two women looked at each other, then fell into each other's arms.

"Sister!" cried the fair lady.

"Charity! Dear Charity!" sobbed Goodwife Partridge.

"Aunt Charity hath come at last," said Comfort softly.

◆ ◆ ◆

Comfort came to the attic chamber early the next morning. "The neighbors be come to see you, Aunt!" she said.

"What wild roars and loud wailing heard I through the night?" asked Aunt Charity. "Some said on the *Fearless* ye have lions here that roar. Is it true, Comfort?"

"Father says some have seen a lion at Cape Ann," replied Comfort. "He hath seen skins of all other beasts save only lions."

"It howled so fierce, it did affright me," Aunt Charity went on. " 'Twas not a lion then?"

"No, Aunt, 'twas not a lion."

With sober face, Comfort glanced at the bed, where lay bright-colored garments with trimmings of lace and embroidery. Aunt Charity picked up several things and together they went down the narrow stairs. Comfort sat silently down on a block in the corner. She took up a red stocking she was knitting.

"My sister, Widow Cummings, gossips," announced Goodwife Partridge proudly.

"It gladdens our hearts to see you!" cried Mistress Seward.

She stepped forward and grasped Aunt Charity's hands in her own. Then came the others, Mistress Hollingworth, Mistress Cartwright, Goodwives Pitkin, Minching, Rogers, Perkins and Lumpkin.

"Tell us news of Old England!" begged the women.

"The grass is green, the flowers bloom bravely, the lark still soars and sings in the heavens," said Aunt Charity softly. She sat down in a chair and continued: "It seems only yesterday I was there in my father's old home in Essex. The roses were a-bloom in the bed beside the gravel path, the figs were ripening along the wall above the kitchen garden, the air was sweet with fragrance . . ."

"I be fair homesick to hear ye tell it!" cried Goodwife Pitkin. "The very words do make my heart beat faster!"

Questions poured thick and fast.

"Eat they still manchets of fine white wheaten bread?" asked Goodwife Rogers. "I did so love manchet bread. Here we eat brown bread, corn meal mixed with rye, or Indian bannock of corn meal only."

"Drink they still swish-swash in Essex, made of drained honeycombs and spice?" asked Goodwife Minching. " 'Twas good to cure the cough and ease the swallowing."

"Have ye been in fair London Town of late?" cried Mistress Hollingworth. "Saw ye the water-bearers? Heard ye the clop-clop of horses' hooves? The noisy street-cries: 'Hassocks for your pews,' 'Sweet lavender,' and 'Cherries ripe'?"

"Ay, ay, gossips!" laughed Widow Cummings. "To all I answer yes. Old England is Old England still, and ever will be!"

The women's eyes filled with tears.

Comfort's hands forgot to knit as she stared and listened.

"Heed thy knitting, daughter!" came the stern reproof from her mother.

Only Mistress Seward stood aloof and asked no questions. After a moment, she broke out: "Why come ye here, Mistress, to prate of the England we hope never to see again? Be ye wishful to make us homesick?"

Silence fell, as friendliness turned to bitterness.

"Homesickness be sinful to indulge in," cried Goody Lumpkin. "It be but weakness. Old England be best forgot."

The others, ashamed now of recent tears, joined in.

"Them that hunger after Old England fall into discontent and die," said Mistress Cartwright.

"Unless they take the scurvy first," added Goodwife Minching in a tone of bitter sadness.

"To fix your eyes on Old England's chimney-pots bringeth on sickness, that we well know," sighed Mistress Hollingworth.

Widow Cummings rose to her feet, astonished. "But would ye then forget the land that bore thee, the land ye love so much?"

"Sister," reproved Goodwife Partridge hastily, "ye have done us a great unkindness to stir up our love for Old England, which we had thought dead. Speak of it no more."

Undisturbed, Widow Cummings opened a small bag and

spread its contents on the table. Comfort's knitting fell to the floor as she ran forward to look.

"Gossips," said Widow Cummings quietly, "I brought thee seeds of herbs from my father's garden in Essex." She put small packets into the women's open palms. "Here's fennel to sharpen the eyes and the brain; rosemary to strengthen the memory; mustard to revive the spirits; lettuce to give peace and rest; borage to bring good cheer; and basil, sweet basil, to chase away sorrowfulness and melancholy. Of all these, I see ye have great need."

The women murmured shamefaced thanks.

Widow Cummings approached Goodwife Partridge. "These be London gloves, embroidered," she said, holding out three pairs. "I brought them for you, sister."

"Oh! Look ye!" "Ah . . . how lovely!" cried the women.

"Comfort!" scolded her mother. "Thy knitting. See ye to it."

The girl went back to her seat and took up her work.

"My hands be coarse and rough," said Goodwife Partridge, holding them out. "Not fitting for fine gloves."

"Here we work hard," murmured Goodwife Rogers.

"Here a woman must not be butter-fingered, sweet-toothed nor faint-hearted," put in Mistress Seward severely.

"For ten long years we've given no thought to gloves and finery," chimed in Goodwife Minching.

"Ye mean it well, sister," said Goodwife Partridge sadly. "But our clothes be old and shabby. Fine gloves become us not."

"Dear sister," cried Widow Cummings eagerly, "have ye forgot the fine apparel ye wore when ye were young?

Remember ye not the fair gown our mother wrought for thy marriage? With embroidered under-petticoat trimmed with silver lace, and great sleeves of taffety, three times slashed?"

"I see it still," said the Goodwife softly, while the women crowded close. "I mind yet the sweet rustle of its silken skirts. 'Twas in the sea-chest we threw overboard to lighten the cargo, on our voyage ten years ago. But we dare not speak of embroidered petticoats here. These gloves . . ."

"Our goodly Magistrate liketh not pride and vain-glory," said Goodwife Rogers.

"Parson Humphrey counselleth us to give our minds and hearts to higher things," said Mistress Seward. "He ever preacheth against intolerable pride in clothes and hair."

"Let me but show thee my mulberry London gown," cried Widow Cummings. "When thy goodly Magistrate and thy goodly Parson see it . . ."

"Oh, sister, wear it not abroad!" Goodwife Partridge's face turned pale. "This be not Old England. Things be different here, as ye will soon enough find out. It fares not well with those who follow after vanity. It betokens a carnal heart."

Goody Lumpkin, who had been standing by the door, now stalked out. "The words I have heard from this newcomer," she shouted back angrily, "be an abomination and a snare of the Devil. I will hear no more."

"She will tell it out abroad." The women shook their heads and whispered. "She is a tale-bearer."

"Are ye then afraid?" cried Widow Cummings boldly. "Why, what evil hath been done?"

After the women took their leave, Goodwife Partridge handed the gloves back to her sister. "These I cannot wear. Nor can you."

"We shall see," said Charity with a smile. She turned to Comfort. "How goes thy knitting, lass? Let me pick up those stitches ye dropped." Comfort handed the stocking over.

The house was quiet after the women left. Thankful returned from the Minchings with a pail of milk. Goodwife Partridge went out the back door and soon returned.

"The gossips stayed full half the morn," she complained. "A waste of precious time. My work is but begun . . ."

"Dost carry thy own water, sister?" asked Charity, astonished.

"Ay!" said Goodwife Partridge, setting down her piggin.

"Ye carry water and do like drudgery?"

"I carry water, too," said Comfort proudly.

"So do I, though some time I spill!" added Thankful.

"Only the poorer sort do that in Old England," said Aunt Charity. "London tankard-bearers and country cottagers. The Indians, they help thee not?"

"They make not good servants," answered Goodwife Partridge. "A wild people they be, difficult to tame."

"I had bought the redemptioner from off the *Fearless,* had I known ye had no servant," said Charity thoughtfully.

"The wicked maid, Aunt? With sinful heart, who came off the boat *in her hair?*" Comfort's eyes opened wide.

"Ay, lass," replied Aunt Charity. "Kindness maketh a good servant of even a wicked girl."

Comfort pondered these words in silence. They sounded

very strange. Goodwife Partridge filled a second piggin and brought it in. She set it on a form by the door.

"Why so much water?" asked her sister.

"We must have water for washing and brewing and cooking. We must have water to drink . . ."

"To drink? Drink ye then water?" asked Aunt Charity in surprise.

"We have little milk." Goodwife Partridge's tone was patient. "Our share is small. Three families, the Minchings, the Sewards and ourselves, share the milk of one cow. God grant there be more, now that the *Fearless* hath brought more cattle. They be sorely needed."

"They be but thin and scrawny beasts," said Gaffer Partridge, who had just come in with the two boys. "And a winter of scanty feeding will not make much milk. Next summer, after they go out to pasture, perhaps we can hope for milk for all."

"We manage right well," added Goodwife Partridge cheerfully, "seeing every family or two hath a spring of sweet waters betwixt them, or the sea by their very door."

"Ye *drink* water?" asked Charity, unbelieving.

"Not salty sea water, but clear, clean spring water," answered her sister. "We have drunk naught else for so long . . ."

"Here, Aunt, take a drink!" Comfort filled a mug and held it to her lips.

Her aunt took a sip, then turned away with a wry face.

"It be not accounted a strange thing here, to drink water!" laughed Goodwife Partridge. "Ye must learn to like it."

"Here ye drink water and do without many delicacies

enjoyed in Old England," said Gaffer Partridge solemnly, as he took a seat by the fireside. "Fountains do not stream forth wine and ale. Woods and rivers are not like butchers' shops or fishmongers' stalls. If thou canst not live without those things, the *Fearless* waits to take thee back whence thou camest. A proud heart, a dainty tooth and an idle hand be here intolerable!"

But Aunt Charity refused to be solemn. She turned to her sister's husband with a twinkle in her eye. "You *like* it then, John? You *like* water?"

Gaffer Partridge smiled. "I dare not prefer it before good beer as some have done," he said, "but any man would choose it before bad beer, whey or buttermilk. It be far different from the water of Old England, being not so sharp, but of a fatter substance. It is thought there can be no better water in the world."

The children gathered round the fireplace.

"The Indians drink water freely," said Seaborn. "They take it up in their two palms and drink at the wrists."

"They drink naught but water," added Comfort. "Never any milk. They keep no cows."

"I gave Know-God a taste of my beer once," said Seaborn, chuckling, "and he spat it out like some vile thing!"

"Yet another sip of sweet water, Aunt?" asked Comfort, holding out the mug invitingly.

"No, no!" laughed Aunt Charity. "Take it away. But one sip for the first day. Life without Old England's ale will indeed be strange."

"We brew molasses beer," said her sister, "when we can get the malt from England."

"There be many new and strange things for each newcomer to learn," said Gaffer Partridge seriously. "A strange but fair land this."

" 'Tis said that those who commend it, do so in strawberry time or when wild roses fill the air with sweet fragrance," laughed Aunt Charity gaily. "But when the winter wind blows chill and bringeth hardship, they close tight their lips and say naught!"

"Despite all hardship, still we say the land is fair," said Gaffer Partridge. "Despite all we suffer, none wishes to return. There be but three serious inconveniences — Indians, wolves and mosquitoes. But these be naught beside that great benefit we came to enjoy — freedom to worship God as we please."

"Mos—kee—toes? What be they?" asked Aunt Charity.

"Creatures that have six legs and live like monsters altogether upon man's flesh!" laughed Gaffer Partridge. "The Governor saith that those who be too delicate to endure the biting of a mosquito should bide at home till they be mosquito-proof. Come summer, ye will make a mosquito's acquaintance and fall a-scratching like the rest of us, I doubt not."

Goodwife Partridge and the children laughed merrily.

"Be they worse than Indians?" asked Aunt Charity.

"Worse than Indians!" The family laughed again.

"Ye have Indians for neighbors?" asked Aunt Charity. "Is it safe then to go abroad?"

"None live in Fair Haven By-the-Sea," answered her sister, "save one, a boy, called Know-God. His family were taken by small-pox and he alone survived. English people brought him here four years ago and Parson Humphrey hath adopted him."

"Wherefore is he called Know-God?"

"When the Indians are put in mind of God, their usual answer is, 'we not know God.' "

"Know-God is fleet of foot and sharp of eye," said Seaborn.

"The Indians eat no salt, they live in mat-covered huts in the woods," explained Gaffer Partridge. "They live off the flesh of deer, bear, moose, raccoon, and fish when they can get naught else. They grow maize and eat *nokechick* — parched meal, powdered."

"They be dangerous?" asked Aunt Charity.

"They be friends when they be friendly," said Gaffer Partridge. "They be enemies when they be unfriendly."

"Your wild beasts be dangerous, too, be they not?" asked Aunt Charity. "I heard unearthly howling in the middle of the night, followed by the shot of a gun. What beast was it, come under my very window?"

No one answered. Aunt Charity looked round at the children's closed lips, then at her sister's.

"Why be ye then so silent? Sister, have ye forbidden the childer to speak? Think ye to spare me? Must not I know the worst soon or late?"

Still no one spoke.

"Comfort telled me 'twas not a lion." She turned to her brother-in-law. "But surely I heard roars and loud wailing, as if wild lions came to life while man slept and took his rest."

Gaffer Partridge glanced at his wife, then answered with a bitter smile: "I took *not* my rest. Ye need not be affrighted of lions. 'Twas a sneaking wolf leaped over our paling fence and snatched a young goat from the pen. We lost the kid, but got the wolf."

"We feared to affright you," said Goodwife Partridge, "on your first night in this new land. I bade the childer hold their tongues."

The children now felt free to speak.

"Poor little kid," said Comfort sadly.

"T'other kid will be lonely," added Thankful.

"We have skinned the wolf already," boasted Seaborn. "His black hide hath great value among the Indians."

"The town pays fifteen shillings bounty as well," added Gaffer Partridge, "to help rid the settlement of the pest."

"We returned but now," piped up little Waitstill, "from hanging our wolf's head on the meeting house door. I will take you to see it tomorrow, Aunt. On the great stone step the blood drippeth red, in great puddles . . ."

"Ugh!" cried Aunt Charity, with distaste. "Mosquitoes, Indians, wolves! A strange land this!"

The children laughed.

◆ ◆ ◆

"Come, sweet childer!" cried Aunt Charity. "The day is sunny and warm. We will go for a stroll. Me-thinks ye have sat still long enough."

Waitstill and Comfort came eagerly, but Thankful sat motionless beside God-be-thanked's cradle.

"I bide here to mind the babe," she said. "Mother is over-busy with the monthly washing. I like not to leave her."

"Thou art a goodly child," said Aunt Charity, patting her on the head. "Another day thy turn will come for a frolic."

"A frolic, Aunt?" asked Thankful soberly. "Better to spend one's days from early morn till set o' sun repenting of one's wickedness in the sight of God. Frolicking — there be no time for that."

"Hear the child preach!" laughed Aunt Charity. "Truly an old head on young shoulders . . ."

"Hush, sister, hush!" begged Goodwife Partridge, from the corner of the large hall, where her back was bent over a wooden tub.

"Ay, but I *shall* speak!" Charity's cheeks flushed pink. "Want ye then no children at all? Want ye to make sober old men and sad-faced women out of babes in their very cradles?"

"We try but to lead godly lives," said Goodwife Partridge severely.

"Come with me, childer!" cried Aunt Charity.

They started out briskly. Aunt Charity wore her London mulberry gown of soft kersey. Below the lace ruffles of the full sleeves, she wore her open-work London gloves. Her cut-work coif showed plainly under her black beaver hat, with its band of pearls. Comfort knew she had never seen anyone so beautiful.

"What ails ye, childer?" Aunt Charity looked down at the two sober-faced children. "Have ye forgot how to ope your mouths and speak? Do you never prattle, babble, cackle? Never frisk and skip about like young lambs? Be not so mannerly, I beg you!"

No words came. The lesson of keeping silence before their elders was well-learned.

"Let us find a high hill," said Aunt Charity, "where we can see naught but the blue sea — that little pond of water which separates us from Old England. I want to look across it and see dear England once more. I feel as if I've been away for years."

"We could pick bayberries," said Comfort shyly. "Black Cloud's squaw makes a useful salve by pressing them to powder . . ."

"But I promised I would take Aunt Charity to see the wolf's head on the meeting house door," interrupted Waitstill. He paused thoughtfully. "But if ye will be affrighted, Aunt, then 'tis best not to go."

"I shall not be affrighted, child," replied Aunt Charity. "I must learn all these new ways. I go with you to see the wolf's head."

"But it maketh me sick to see blood," cried Comfort, in distress.

"I be fair 'shamed of you!" scolded Waitstill. "Ye can wait then round the corner, while I show it to Aunt Charity. 'Twill not make thee sick to stomach, Aunt?"

"No, child," said Aunt Charity stoutly. "We go first to the hill, then to the meeting house. Tell me more about these Indians of yours."

"Ye have never seen an Indian, then?" laughed Waitstill.

"Of course she hasn't," replied Comfort. "Dark of skin and black of hair they be. They dress in deer-hide, tanned and fringed."

"Look ye now!" cried Waitstill. "There cometh Black Cloud and his squaw."

A tall Indian man, with a skin slung over one shoulder, appeared with his fat, dumpy squaw at his heels. The woman carried a load of beaver hides on her back.

"They be bound for the trading house, to barter their furs for needful supplies," explained Comfort.

Aunt Charity's eyes followed the pair. "Be they dangerous?"

"Not very," replied Comfort. "They come oft to our house. Black Cloud accounts himself my father's best friend, having once saved his life."

Walking on, they came to a broad stretch of bare hill, below the fort, where among scattering rocks, bayberries grew in silver clusters. Comfort gathered up her apron and the children ran happily about, picking. Aunt Charity stood silent and thoughtful, gazing across the open sea. Suddenly she realized the children were shouting. They *can* shout, after all, she thought to herself.

Then words smote her ear: "Run, Aunt, run! Make haste, Aunt, make haste!"

A moment of panic seized her, as she saw a herd of wild animals rush toward her. Over the rise of a great sand dune they came, egged on by a shower of sharp stones thrown by a long-legged boy and a group of dark-skinned, scantily clad children. Aunt Charity gathered up her petticoats and ran with all speed. Comfort and Waitstill ran close beside her. Comfort's apron fell from her grasp and the bayberries scattered. In the shelter of a huge boulder they stopped and drew breath.

"Be they wolves?" cried Aunt Charity, trembling.

"Wolves!" laughed Waitstill. "Not wolves but swine. Know-God and the Indian children drive the swine off the beach — the tide be out."

The galloping hogs rushed madly across the rocky field, then down the hill, scattered helter-skelter among the narrow lanes of the village.

"The Indian women come to the beach at low tide to gather clams," explained Comfort. "Clams are a dainty with them for eating."

"The swine come too," added Waitstill. "They turn up clams with their snouts and eat them."

" 'Tis ever a fight between Indians and hogs," Comfort went on, "to see who gets the most clams."

"But why keep ye not your hogs in pens?" asked Aunt Charity.

"There be naught to feed them," replied Comfort. "They must forage for their own food."

"Wherefore they grow bold," added Waitstill. "The hogs rush up to eat when Mother throws her slops out by the door. They dig ditches in the streets and lie down and rest there when tired. They fight fiercely with dogs and chase people indoors."

"Hogs!" said Aunt Charity. "Yet another evil to contend with."

"Hogs?" cried Comfort. "We pay no heed to hogs . . ."

"Except to get out of their way!" added Aunt Charity, laughing.

"Now go we to the meeting house," announced Waitstill.

"Ay! To the meeting house!" replied Aunt Charity, taking his hand.

On the downward slope of the hill, they passed a rude shelter, a cave dug into the bank of earth, held up with wooden spars and a covering of turf. Not far away were three crude hovels, their arched hickory framework covered over with rush mats or pine bark securely lashed. Each had a stone fireplace set at the end, with clay-daubed chimney.

"That one is called a dug-out," said Waitstill, pointing to the cave, "being dug out of the hill."

"The others be English wigwams," said Comfort.

Aunt Charity shuddered. "Do people live here?"

"The English men built them when first they came here to live," explained Comfort. "Now that we have better houses, with two rooms, a loft and thatched roofs, these be abandoned."

"But I see smoke coming from the chimneys," said Aunt Charity.

"Doubtless some of the newcomers from the *Fearless* live here till better houses be built," said Comfort.

Aunt Charity turned her eyes away.

The path followed the beach where the Indian women and children could be seen, unmolested now by swine, digging clams. The path wandered past the salt works where two salt-workers were evaporating salty sea water in shallow pans, and along by the fish flakes where rows of fish lay on wooden racks, spread out to dry in the sun. Then it came again to the village.

Aunt Charity looked about her. She saw the blacksmith shop with glowing forge, the brick works, and then facing the village green, two houses larger than the others, having two stories instead of one.

"That be the Magistrate's house," said Comfort, "and this the ordinary, Landlord Cluffe, proprietor."

" 'Tis called the Blue Anchor," said Waitstill. "There be the anchor pictured on the sign."

"Have ye then no shops, no merchants?" asked Aunt Charity. "Is there then no place to buy?"

Waitstill shook his head. "Only the trading house," said Comfort.

A half-grown girl came swiftly up behind. She rushed forward and planted herself before them.

"Who art thou, lass?" asked Aunt Charity. "Why block ye my path?"

The girl wore no coif and her hair hung wild and loose. She was dressed in servant's garb, sad-colored gown of linsey-woolsey, with kerchief and apron of calico. Her hand went to her bare head.

"My coif . . . I lost it, I ran so hard . . . to catch thee . . ."

"Who art thou? Why do ye molest me?" asked Aunt Charity again.

"Patience Tucker, if it please ye, Ma'am. Mind ye not Patty?" cried the girl. "Patience Tucker, ye redemptioner, whom ye 'friended on the *Fearless?*"

"Patty!" cried Aunt Charity, delighted. "I didn't know thee. So neat and clean and handsome ye look! Art well disposed? Good home, good mistress, food to eat, all else? A comfort 'tis to . . ."

"Nay, Ma'am!" Patty's voice was loud and coarse. "She beats me, Ma'am. I hate her. I came to tell ye, Ma'am. Take me away, Ma'am!"

"But, Patty, art trying hard, as ye promised, to be a good servant?"

"She beats me, Ma'am. I hate her, Ma'am, I'll run away . . ."

"Patience Tucker, listen ye to me!" Aunt Charity's voice was solemn and stern. "Ye gave me your word ye would be a dutiful servant, do as ye were bid . . ."

"She beats me, Ma'am! Oh, kind friend, if ye love me, take me away from her!"

"I cannot, Patty," replied Aunt Charity. "Those who are bound must obey. Your master and mistress have paid for your passage. You must repay them with five years' work. There is no other way. Go to your mistress and do your duty, or they will send you back to England sure."

The girl turned sorrowfully away.

"Come not abroad in your hair, Patty. Ye'd best find your coif and put it on, lest thy mistress chide thee," added Aunt Charity kindly.

"What a wicked, sinful girl. . . ," began Comfort.

"Know ye why she is wicked, lass?" asked Aunt Charity. " 'Tis only because she has never known love."

The door of the ordinary opened and a tall man stepped out. He wore a steeple-crowned hat and a full black cape that switched about his knees. He paused, waiting till the group came up.

"The Magistrate, Aunt, 'tis the Magistrate!" Whispering, Comfort clutched her aunt's hand and pulled her back.

But Aunt Charity loosed her hold and advanced smiling.

"Widow Cummings, I believe," said the Magistrate.

Aunt Charity bowed her head a trifle.

"A topish hat, with a fair pearl hat-band, if I mistake not!" said the Magistrate, frowning.

"Ay, good sir! Pearl!" Widow Cummings lifted her chin.

The man's glance left the hat, descended downward, ignoring her bright eyes and flushed cheeks. "Thou hast whalebone in the bodice of thy gown, hast not?"

"Ay, good sir! Whalebone!"

His gaze continued downward. "Gown of mulberry kersey, is't not?"

"Ay, good sir! Mulberry kersey!" Aunt Charity smiled.

"And open-work London gloves?"

"Ay, good sir! Of the latest fashion!"

Down to the ground went the Magistrate's eyes. "Corked shoes, if I mistake not!"

"Ay, good sir!" laughed Aunt Charity gaily. "With woman's gear thou showest no mean acquaintance."

The Magistrate's face reddened.

"And if it please you, good sir," Aunt Charity went on, "I have come well-prepared for New England's biting winter. To keep my ears warm, I have a blue velvet hood!"

But the Magistrate saw no occasion for levity. He frowned and his voice was harsh. "I admonish you not only for flaunting unseemly apparel, but for boasting thereof. Pride and vain-glory — these be of Satan. I hereby warn you lest thy sins bring punishment upon thy head and dishonor upon thy God."

Widow Cummings lowered her eyes. "I should indeed be sorry, good sir, if such came to pass, for I am a godly woman," she said in a contrite voice. "I do but wear such apparel as I have formerly been wont to wear in Old England. This gown is one my mother bequeathed to me. She, in turn, inherited it from her mother. The material is of the best quality, made to endure. If I should discard the apparel I brought with me from Old England, where may I obtain plainer clothing to replace it? You will perhaps direct me to the nearest shop and help me make a suitable selection?"

A group of people had collected. Among them, Widow

Cummings recognized two of her first callers, Goodwives Minching and Lumpkin.

The Magistrate stammered uncertainly. "We have yet no shop . . ."

"No shop? How then can I buy?"

"The seamen ofttimes bring goods to sell . . ."

"Ay, I saw the cheap and shoddy pieces they brought on the *Fearless* and heard what exorbitant prices they asked," said Widow Cummings. "Is that the only merchandising you allow in your fair town?"

The Magistrate coughed. "There be shops in Boston Town . . ."

"And thirty miles to walk to get there," added Widow Cummings. "If then I cannot buy, perhaps I can find wool and have it spun and woven into a piece of enduring cloth?"

"We have only a few sheep," answered the Magistrate. "We expect more in the spring — but as yet no wool to sell. The Master weaver I sent for died on the voyage . . ."

"What then can I do?" asked Widow Cummings.

"Wear what you have, but see ye flaunt it not," growled the Magistrate. "For the flaunting of gaudy apparel, ye can be presented at Court. Take heed."

He stalked away angrily. The women passed by without a word. Aunt Charity took the two children by the hand and started to cross the village green.

"He liked not thy mulberry London gown," said Comfort sadly. " 'Twas just as Mother said. But I like it well, Aunt."

"And so do I," added Waitstill.

Aunt Charity did not trust herself to speak.

"There be the stocks!" cried Waitstill, pointing.

"And there the pillory and whipping post!" added Comfort. "They be engines of punishment for wrong-doers. Have they then stocks and whipping posts in Old England?"

"Ay!" replied Aunt Charity sadly. "In Old England there be wrong-doing too."

Soon they came to the meeting house at the opposite end of the green. It was a one-story building with a thatched roof and a row of five windows, fastened with strong batten shutters, on each side.

Comfort ran to the far corner to wait.

"Our wolf!" cried Waitstill, pointing proudly to the grim head hung on the blood-stained door.

Aunt Charity looked, for look she must to prove herself not faint-hearted. Then quickly she turned her eyes away.

"Come, childer, we go home now," she said quietly. "We have seen our wolf."

◆ ◆ ◆

The day was cold and blustery. A great fire burned on the Partridge hearth, sending bright sparks up the yawning chimney. Iron pots swung on chains and trammels, hung from the great green-wood lugpole which stretched from ledge to ledge.

Aunt Charity sat on the settle in the warm chimney corner with Comfort beside her. From the work-box on her lap, she took out her needle and silver thimble. She began to embroider cut-work on a strip of fine white Holland cloth.

"What is't, Aunt?" asked Comfort.

"A new coif," said Aunt Charity. She slipped off her cap

and held the dainty white strip round her face. "Look ye! Is't not handsome?"

"I like it well," said Comfort shyly. "Is't hard to do, the cut-work?"

"Not when thy fingers have learnt mastery," said Aunt Charity.

"Could I then . . . could I have a cut-work coif?"

"Comfort!" called her mother suddenly from the lean-to at the rear. "Fetch here those river rushes. Don thy darkest green apron. Then come, scour the pewter well with sand."

The girl ran to do her mother's bidding.

Goodwife Partridge's words came faintly through the half-open door: "Think not of 'broidered coifs. Have I not told thee oft, daughter, that only a sinful heart longs after vanity?"

"Hath Aunt Charity then a sinful heart?"

The door went swiftly shut and Charity heard no more.

She went over her work thoughtfully, her needle flashing in the firelight. The outer door opened and she looked up with a start. There stood a dark-skinned, black-haired woman, dressed in deerskin clothing. The woman looked at her intently, then came forward and placed a carved maple bowl in her hands. Her seamed face broke into a broad smile, as she made a few strange sounds.

An Indian squaw! Charity's heart began to pound as she stared at the strange creature. She saw a girdle of blue and white beads about the woman's waist, bracelets on neck and arms, and links hung in her ears. Then she stared at the black eyes again. She tried to call for help, but no words came. She tried to get up and run, but she could not rise from her chair.

"Black Cloud take Knife Man's red coat," said the squaw. "Red coat no good in forest."

Charity's face turned white.

"He need net and fish-hooks and such toys," the squaw went on angrily. "Need pair of knives, and grindstone to keep them sharp. But he want Knife Man's red coat." She shook her head dismally as she squatted on the hearthstone.

Charity managed to rise. She made haste to the lean-to. "Indians . . . Indians. . . ," she gasped.

"Be not affrighted," said her sister. " 'Tis only Black Cloud's squaw — come out from the forest."

"She talks of knives. . . ," said Charity, trembling.

"Their word for English man is Knife Man," exclaimed Goodwife Partridge. "They never saw knives till the New English men came."

"She gave me this bowl," said Charity.

"Those dainty bowls they prize highly," commented her sister. "But such gifts come more from habit than friendship."

"Ye trust her not?" asked Charity.

"Ye heard what John said. When they be friends, they be friendly. But we must ever be on our guard, lest they turn overnight into enemies."

"She gave me this bowl," said Charity, rubbing its smooth sides lovingly. "She hath an honest look."

"Ay!" assented her sister. "Yet we can never be sure what they are thinking."

Goodwife Partridge came in and talked to the squaw.

"What said she? Is't English she speaketh?" asked Charity.

"A strange English, until your ears grow accustomed to it. Black Cloud hath given all his beaver furs in trade for an

English man's red coat!" replied Goodwife Partridge, with a smile. "Small wonder she is cross. She says they came for needful tools instead."

"Hath she ever done you harm?" asked Charity.

"No, on the contrary, she hath helped us oft," replied her sister. "When first we came, she showed us where to gather wild foods in the woods, how to brew herbs and pound roots, how to make sweet-smelling and potent teas. She is accounted some sort of witch or doctor among her people, the Massachusetts Indians. She knows many cures."

"And yet you trust her not!" added Charity.

She sat down and resumed her embroidery. Now and then she lifted her scissors, which hung from her belt by a bright red ribbon, and snipped bits of cloth away. Goodwife Partridge brought her knitting and sat down beside her sister.

"Look ye and learn why I trust her not," cried Goodwife Partridge in a low voice. "Thy shining needle hath caught her eye. She looketh with envy upon thy bright scissors. Guard well thy needle and scissors, if ye want not to lose them."

"She would take them?" asked Aunt Charity.

"Ay! The Indians take whatever they can lay hands on. Light-fingered they be. We keep close watch always."

"But she hath an honest look . . ." Charity went on with her embroidery, now and then resting her glance on the woman.

Her scouring finished, Comfort replaced her soiled apron with a white one and came back to Aunt Charity's side. Thankful returned from the Minchings with the pail of milk. The boys came bouncing in, full of lively spirits, but upon the threshold changed at once into quiet, good-mannered lads.

God-be-thanked toddled about the hall, his apron full of rye drop cakes fresh from the oven. He passed them out one by one with a solemn air. Unafraid he advanced to the Indian squaw and placed a cake in her open palm.

The door opened and Black Cloud, dressed in his new red doublet, bow in hand and quiver on his back, came in. His face was dark and ugly, made more fearsome by tattooed designs upon his cheeks and a long lock of black hair hanging on one side of his head. Carved bone pendants in the shape of beasts dangled from his ears. Blue and white wampum beads hung round his neck and a girdle of the same encircled his waist. With a nod and a grunt, he squatted on the hearth beside Owl Woman, his squaw.

Goodwife Partridge continued her knitting and Charity her cut-work. Soon Gaffer Partridge returned. He spoke to the Indians, then sat down in a chair by the fire.

"Black Cloud sit in Lumpkin house," began the Indian. "Lumpkin squaw shout thunder words."

"Goody Lumpkin's been scolding her husband again," explained Goodwife Partridge. She turned to the Indian. "You eat dinner Lumpkin house, too?" she asked.

"No eat," said Black Cloud, shaking his head. "Lumpkin squaw not cook, she make big noise with her mouth. She shout loud to her man: Nannana Nannana Nannana Nan! Lumpkin one great fool to let her talk so. He not beat her good when she abuse him with her loud tongue. He say no word, he nimble of foot to run away. She chase Lumpkin out of house, she . . ."

"Chased you out, too?"

"She chase Black Cloud out too," he admitted.

The two women smiled.

Black Cloud saw the smile and rose slowly to his feet. Turning to Gaffer Partridge, he pointed his thumb at the two white women.

"Lazy squaws!" he snorted. "English man much fool, for spoiling good working creatures. Partridge much fool to let them sit in house with needles instead of digging in field."

Goodwife Partridge and Aunt Charity smiled.

"English man's ways be different," said Gaffer Partridge.

His outburst over, Black Cloud squatted down again.

The evening meal could not wait forever. Indians or no, they must eat. Luckily the potful of bean-porridge simmering over the fire was ample. Goodwife Partridge rose to her feet, stirred the mixture, then laid the table and brought out large flat loaves of brown bread.

"Soon we eat," said Waitstill, smiling. "Be ye hungry?"

"Ay!" nodded both the Indians.

Supper ready, the elders took their chairs and the children their places standing. Gaffer Partridge said Grace:

"O Lord, who givest thy creatures for our food,
Herbs, beasts, birds, fish and other gifts of thine,
Bless these thy gifts, that they may do us good,
And we may live, to praise thy name divine.
And when the time is come this life to end:
Vouchsafe our souls to heaven may ascend."

Comfort and Seaborn looked questioningly at their mother, who gave a slight nod. Comfort went to the dresser, brought two trenchers which her father filled with hot bean porridge, and took them to the Indians. Seaborn broke brown bread in pieces and thrust them into the Indians' hands. They ate greedily, with many grunts, then held out their trenchers for more.

"Didst get thy pair of knives, and grindstone to keep them sharp?" asked Seaborn.

Black Cloud growled and shook his head. Then he turned on his squaw and began scolding her in their own language. Obediently she rose and left the house. He took out his pipe and began to smoke.

Charity looked at her sister.

"He telleth her to go home and work," explained Goodwife Partridge in a low voice. "So do they ever order their wives about."

"Will he never go?" asked Charity.

"Not till he's a mind to," answered Gaffer Partridge. "He's a lazy dog, he rests while Owl Woman works."

"Why not order him out if you want him not here?"

"We must keep friendship with the Indians at whatever cost," replied Gaffer Partridge. "Besides, I be forever in his debt. Once when Giles Pitkin and I were out on a hunting expedition, we lost our way in the wilderness. After wandering for two days we came on Black Cloud who led us to his lodging, fed our starving bodies and ministered to our sickness. After we were well again, he feasted us on the haunch of a fat bear. Then, in return for a fourpenny whittle (or fringed shawl), he conducted us through the unbeaten bushy ways for twenty miles, back home again. Ay! We be forever in his debt. I cannot order him out of my house." He paused, then added: "Let us give God thanks:

O Lord our God, we yield thee praise,
For this thy gracious store;
Praying that we may have the grace
To keep thy laws and lore.
And when this life shall flit away,
Grant us to live with Thee for aye."

Comfort and Thankful made haste to stack the trenchers and scour them. Dusk had fallen and the room was in semi-darkness. Suddenly an unexpected noise came from the lean-to. A metal object of some kind fell to the floor with a noisy clatter.

"What is't? The billy-goat?" cried Seaborn anxiously.

"Mayhap 'tis another wolf," cried Waitstill, in excitement, "come now to eat up t'other kid! Make haste to shoot him, father, so we will have two wolf-heads hanging on the meeting house door!"

"Hush, son! Speak not!" scolded Gaffer John.

Comfort clutched God-be-thanked to her breast, and Thankful ran trembling to hide her face in her mother's apron. Goodwife Partridge's eyes never once left the crouching Indian on the hearth.

"Why, what fear ye?" cried Aunt Charity boldly. "Let's ope the door and see what 'tis!" She stepped briskly to the rear door and flung it open wide.

A strange scene met her eyes and the eyes of the family who crowded round — all but Goodwife Partridge, who kept close watch on Black Cloud. A brass kettle had fallen to the floor. It had fallen from a roof-hung shelf.

"What made the kettle fall?" cried Waitstill excitedly.

The answer was plain. A bag of meal, lying now upon the floor, had pushed the empty kettle off the hanging shelf. There, scattered at their feet, sprawling out from the bag's open mouth lay a spreading circle of pale yellow corn meal.

"But what made the bag of meal fall down?" asked Waitstill.

Gaffer Partridge rushed to take his gun from its place over the mantel. Seaborn ran through the lean-to and out the back door. Soon he returned, pulling Black Cloud's sullen and angry squaw behind him.

"*Who* made the bag fall down?" shouted Seaborn angrily. "Owl Woman! 'Twas she who tried to steal our corn! I catched her just in time, ere she scuttled off to the forest. Look ye! Her back is covered with corn dust, her hair is covered too — the bag of meal fell full on her! Shall I not call the Constable?"

Black Cloud rose leisurely from the hearthstone and came out, followed by Goodwife Partridge.

"She stole our corn!" cried Waitstill, pointing.

"No, son!" said Gaffer John sharply. "She stole it not. The corn is still here. The brass kettle hath betrayed her."

"But what matters that? If the corn be still here 'tis through no fault of her own," cried Goodwife Partridge, whose patience was now at an end. "Have we not repaid these Indians with constant kindness? See what good comes thereof!"

Gaffer Partridge agreed. He spoke angrily to the squaw: "Ye tried to steal our corn, but the Lord hath found ye out! 'Twas the Lord who threw the brass kettle to the floor, to betray your wanton sin! Think ye, ye can conceal your wicked theft from the all-seeing eye of God?"

Black Cloud took up the accusation. "Beat her for stealing white man's corn," he cried. "Indians got plenty corn, not need to steal from white man, no. Beat her!"

Bewildered, Owl Woman looked about. Then her eyes rested on the strange new woman with the fair white skin. She ran to Aunt Charity, leaned over and kissed her hand.

"Wait a moment," said Aunt Charity. "I will have words with her. Comfort, come ye here, and tell me what she saith."

Charity, Comfort and the squaw went out by the paling fence. It was nearly dark now. After a few moments they returned.

"She says the English men's swine dug up the Indians' winter cache and ate much corn, which they had saved to eat in winter. She says Black Cloud bade her take corn from the English men, as much as the swine did eat. If she obey him not, he will beat her. He saith the corn rightfully belongs to the Indians — as much as the swine did eat. She speaks the truth. She is an honest woman."

When Aunt Charity finished, there was silence for a while, then Goodwife Partridge broke out: "That's like him! Deceitful, dishonest, not to be trusted . . . teaching her to do his thieving . . ."

"Shall I call the Constable?" cried Seaborn.

"Get you gone from my house, get you gone!" Gaffer Partridge shouted to the Indians in righteous anger.

"But, brother-in-the-law John!" cried Aunt Charity hastily. "Have you not telled me we must keep friendship with the Indians at whatever cost? Would you not sacrifice one bag of meal to keep such friendship? And have you not told me that Black Cloud saved thy life, fed thee when thou wast starving, brought thee to his home and nursed thy sickness? Dost now repay his good with evil, and order him from thy house?"

Gaffer Partridge's anger faded as suddenly as it came. He dropped his head in shame.

Then he walked over to Black Cloud and grasped him by both hands. "Friend!" he said. "Thou and thine are ever welcome to my house and to all that is therein. Ask ye for aught ye wish — even if it be corn — and it is yours."

Author Biographies

Walter D. Edmonds (1903-1998) claimed that he never really wrote books for children, but rather books for adults and children who like to read. His first novel, ***The Matchlock Gun***, a story about frontier survival in America during the eighteenth century, won the Newbery Medal in 1942. He was fond of using the Boonville area of the Mohawk Valley in New York as a setting for his novels, and one of them, ***Bert Breen's Barn,*** won the National Book Award and the Christopher Award in 1976.

Edmonds wrote about strong characters who are determined to succeed despite the obstacles they must face. He wrote more than twenty-five novels, including the famous ***Drums along the Mohawk,*** another account of America as it struggled to expand into the frontier.

Born in Boonville, New York, he studied at Harvard University and later returned there to take a position on the Board of Overseers. He lived in Concord, Massachusetts, until his death.

◆ ◆ ◆

Charles J. Finger (1867-1941) was born in Sussex, England. His parents came to the United States in 1887, but he remained in England until 1890, when he joined a ship's crew and sailed for Chile, where he jumped ship. Finger worked herding sheep and guiding tours of the birds of Tierra del Fuego, among other things. By 1896, Finger was a sheep herder in San Angelo, Texas, where he became a U.S. citizen. He married a sheep rancher's daughter, Eleanor Ferguson, with whom he had five children.

Finger founded a music school; wrote newspaper articles; was a railroad general foreman, a railroad company auditor, company director, and general manager; and a magazine editor and publisher. Having lived in Texas, New Mexico, and Ohio, Finger settled in Fayetteville, Arkansas, in 1920 and lived there until his death in 1941.

A frequent traveler, Finger won the Newbery Medal in 1925

for *Tales from Silver Lands,* a collection of South American fantasies, from which our selections are taken. He also won the Longmans Juvenile Fiction Award in 1929 for his book *Courageous Companions.* Finger was the author of more than sixty books of adventure and biography.

◆ ◆ ◆

Jean Craighead George (1919-) received a Newbery Honor Book award in 1960 for *My Side of the Mountain,* her story of a thirteen-year-old boy's decision to live in the wilderness for a year and survive on whatever he finds there. But it was her incredible story of a thirteen-year-old girl who was adopted by a wolf pack in *Julie of the Wolves* that won her the Newbery Medal in 1973. Julie and the wolves would appear in other books.

George uses intensively researched information for her nature books, writing about nature with an impassioned yet unjudging eye. Her more than seventy novels for children and adults are filled with the details that make up the everyday life of an animal, whether it be a raccoon, mountain lion, or horned owl. She has also written several nonfiction books, including a collection of natural food recipes, and several walking tour books of New York State.

George, born in Washington, D.C., has had a varied and impressive career. Following her studies at Pennsylvania State University, Louisiana State University, and the University of Michigan at Ann Arbor, she was a reporter for the International News Service and *The Washington Post.* From 1969 to 1982, she served as a staff writer, then a roving editor for *Reader's Digest.* In 1944 she married John Lothar George and raised a family consisting of one daughter and two sons. She currently lives in Chappaqua, New York.

◆ ◆ ◆

Lois Lenski (1893-1974) is known primarily for her series of middle-school books detailing the lives of everyday American families. Volumes such as *Cotton in My Sack, Shoo-Fly Girl,* and

San Francisco Boy, respectively, detail the fictional lives of a Southern sharecropper girl, a Pennsylvania Amish girl, and a Chinese-American boy living in San Francisco. In 1946, the Newbery Medal was awarded to Lenski's book, ***Strawberry Girl,*** which tells about a girl named Birdie and her family as they start a strawberry farm in Florida. These books are made all the more real by the author's exhaustive research into the lives of these various regional groups of people, often including visits to see their day-to-day activities in person.

Born in Springfield, Ohio, Lenski earned a B.S. in education from Ohio State University, then went on to study at the Art Students' League in New York and the prestigious Westminster School of Art in London. Right after school, she married the artist Arthur Covey and raised their son and two stepchildren with him until his death in 1960. Her artwork garnered her several single artist shows, notably a display of oil paintings in the Weyhe Gallery and a watercolors show in the Ferargils Gallery, both in New York. She also was included in group art shows at the Pennsylvania Water Color Show and the New York Water Color Show.

During her lifetime, she wrote more than one hundred books of stories, poetry, and plays, the majority of them illustrated by her as well. Her autobiography, ***Journey into Childhood,*** was finished two years before her death.

Newbery Award-Winning Books

2001

WINNER:
A Year Down Yonder by Richard Peck

HONOR BOOKS:
Hope Was Here by Joan Bauer
The Wanderer by Sharon Creech
Because of Winn-Dixie by Kate DiCamillo
Joey Pigza Loses Control by Jack Gantos

2000

WINNER:
Bud, Not Buddy by Christopher Paul Curtis

HONOR BOOKS:
Getting Near to Baby by Audrey Couloumbis
Our Only May Amelia by Jennifer L. Holm
26 Fairmount Avenue by Tomie dePaola

1999

WINNER:
Holes by Louis Sachar

HONOR BOOK:
A Long Way from Chicago by Richard Peck

1998

WINNER:
Out of the Dust by Karen Hesse

HONOR BOOKS:
Ella Enchanted by Gail Carson Levine
Lily's Crossing by Patricia Reilly Giff
Wringer by Jerry Spinelli

1997

WINNER:
The View from Saturday by E.L. Konigsburg

HONOR BOOKS:
Belle Prater's Boy by Ruth White
A Girl Named Disaster by Nancy Farmer
Moorchild by Eloise McGraw
The Thief by Megan Whalen Turner

1996

WINNER:
The Midwife's Apprentice by Karen Cushman

HONOR BOOKS:
The Great Fire by Jim Murphy
The Watsons Go to Birmingham — 1963 by Christopher Paul Curtis
What Jamie Saw by Carolyn Coman
Yolanda's Genius by Carol Fenner

1995

WINNER:
Walk Two Moons by Sharon Creech

HONOR BOOKS:
Catherine, Called Birdy by Karen Cushman
The Ear, the Eye, and the Arm by Nancy Farmer

1994

WINNER:
The Giver by Lois Lowry

HONOR BOOKS:
Crazy Lady by Jane Leslie Conly
Dragon's Gate by Laurence Yep
Eleanor Roosevelt: A Life of Discovery by Russell Freedman

1993

WINNER:
Missing May by Cynthia Rylant

HONOR BOOKS:

The Dark-thirty: Southern Tales of the Supernatural by Patricia McKissack

Somewhere in the Darkness by Walter Dean Myers

What Hearts by Bruce Brooks

1992

WINNER:

Shiloh by Phyllis Reynolds Naylor

HONOR BOOKS:

Nothing But the Truth: A Documentary Novel by Avi

The Wright Brothers: How They Invented the Airplane by Russell Freedman

1991

WINNER:

Maniac Magee by Jerry Spinelli

HONOR BOOK:

The True Confessions of Charlotte Doyle by Avi

1990

WINNER:

Number the Stars by Lois Lowry

HONOR BOOKS:

Afternoon of the Elves by Janet Taylor Lisle

Shabanu, Daughter of the Wind by Suzanne Fisher Staples

The Winter Room by Gary Paulsen

1989

WINNER:

Joyful Noise: Poems for Two Voices by Paul Fleischman

HONOR BOOKS:

In the Beginning: Creation Stories from around the World by Virginia Hamilton

Scorpions by Walter Dean Myers

1988

WINNER:

Lincoln: A Photobiography by Russell Freedman

HONOR BOOKS:

After the Rain by Norma Fox Mazer

Hatchet by Gary Paulsen

1987

WINNER:

The Whipping Boy by Sid Fleischman

HONOR BOOKS:

A Fine White Dust by Cynthia Rylant

On My Honor by Marion Dane Bauer

Volcano: The Eruption and Healing of Mount St. Helens by Patricia Lauber

1986

WINNER:

Sarah, Plain and Tall by Patricia MacLachlan

HONOR BOOKS:

Commodore Perry in the Land of the Shogun by Rhonda Blumberg

Dogsong by Gary Paulsen

1985

WINNER:

The Hero and the Crown by Robin McKinley

HONOR BOOKS:

Like Jake and Me by Mavis Jukes

The Moves Make the Man by Bruce Brooks

One-Eyed Cat by Paula Fox

1984

WINNER:

Dear Mr. Henshaw by Beverly Cleary

HONOR BOOKS:

The Sign of the Beaver by Elizabeth George Speare

A Solitary Blue by Cynthia Voigt

Sugaring Time by Kathryn Lasky

The Wish Giver: Three Tales of Coven Tree by Bill Brittain

1983

WINNER:

Dicey's Song by Cynthia Voigt

HONOR BOOKS:

The Blue Sword by Robin McKinley

Doctor DeSoto by William Steig

Graven Images by Paul Fleischman

Homesick: My Own Story by Jean Fritz

Sweet Whispers, Brother Rush by Virginia Hamilton

1982

WINNER:

A Visit to William Blake's Inn: Poems for Innocent and Experienced Travelers by Nancy Willard

HONOR BOOKS:

Ramona Quimby, Age 8 by Beverly Cleary

Upon the Head of the Goat: A Childhood in Hungary 1939-1944 by Aranka Siegal

1981

WINNER:

Jacob Have I Loved by Katherine Paterson

HONOR BOOKS:

The Fledgling by Jane Langton

A Ring of Endless Light by Madeleine L'Engle

1980

WINNER:

A Gathering of Days: A New England Girl's Journal, 1830-1832 by Joan W. Blos

HONOR BOOK:

The Road from Home: The Story of an Armenian Girl by David Kherdian

1979

WINNER:

The Westing Game by Ellen Raskin

HONOR BOOK:

The Great Gilly Hopkins by Katherine Paterson

1978

WINNER:

Bridge to Terabithia by Katherine Paterson

HONOR BOOKS:

Anpao: An American Indian Odyssey by Jamake Highwater

Ramona and Her Father by Beverly Cleary

1977

WINNER:

Roll of Thunder, Hear My Cry by Mildred D. Taylor

HONOR BOOKS:

Abel's Island by William Steig

A String in the Harp by Nancy Bond

1976

WINNER:

The Grey King by Susan Cooper

HONOR BOOKS:

Dragonwings by Laurence Yep

The Hundred Penny Box by Sharon Bell Mathis

1975

WINNER:

M.C. Higgins, the Great by Virginia Hamilton

HONOR BOOKS:

Figgs & Phantoms by Ellen Raskin

My Brother Sam Is Dead
by James Lincoln Collier
and Christopher Collier

The Perilous Gard
by Elizabeth Marie Pope

Philip Hall Likes Me, I Reckon Maybe
by Bette Greene

1974

WINNER:
The Slave Dancer by Paula Fox

HONOR BOOK:
The Dark Is Rising by Susan Cooper

1973

WINNER:
Julie of the Wolves
by Jean Craighead George

HONOR BOOKS:
Frog and Toad Together
by Arnold Lobel

The Upstairs Room by Johanna Reiss

The Witches of Worm
by Zilpha Keatley Snyder

1972

WINNER:
Mrs. Frisby and the Rats of NIMH
by Robert C. O'Brien

HONOR BOOKS:
Annie and the Old One
by Miska Miles

The Headless Cupid
by Zilpha Keatley Snyder

Incident at Hawk's Hill
by Allan W. Eckert

The Planet of Junior Brown
by Virginia Hamilton

The Tombs of Atuan
by Ursula K. Le Guin

1971

WINNER:
Summer of the Swans by Betsy Byars

HONOR BOOKS:
Enchantress from the Stars
by Sylvia Louise Engdahl

Knee Knock Rise by Natalie Babbitt

Sing Down the Moon by Scott O'Dell

1970

WINNER:
Sounder by William H. Armstrong

HONOR BOOKS:
Journey Outside by Mary Q. Steele

The Many Ways of Seeing: An Introduction to the Pleasures of Art
by Janet Gaylord Moore

Our Eddie by Sulamith Ish-Kishor

1969

WINNER:
The High King by Lloyd Alexander

HONOR BOOKS:
To Be a Slave by Julius Lester

When Shlemiel Went to Warsaw and Other Stories
by Isaac Bashevis Singer

1968

WINNER:
From the Mixed-Up Files of Mrs. Basil E. Frankweiler
by E.L. Konigsburg

HONOR BOOKS:
The Black Pearl
by Scott O'Dell

The Egypt Game
by Zilpha Keatley Snyder

The Fearsome Inn
by Isaac Bashevis Singer

Jennifer, Hecate, Macbeth, William McKinley, and Me, Elizabeth
by E.L. Konigsburg

1967

WINNER:
Up a Road Slowly by Irene Hunt

HONOR BOOKS:

The Jazz Man by Mary Hays Weik

The King's Fifth by Scott O'Dell

Zlateh the Goat and Other Stories by Isaac Bashevis Singer

1966

WINNER:

I, Juan de Pareja by Elizabeth Borton de Trevino

HONOR BOOKS:

The Animal Family by Randall Jarrell

The Black Cauldron by Lloyd Alexander

The Noonday Friends by Mary Stolz

1965

WINNER:

Shadow of a Bull by Maia Wojciechowska

HONOR BOOK:

Across Five Aprils by Irene Hunt

1964

WINNER:

It's Like This, Cat by Emily Neville

HONOR BOOKS:

The Loner by Ester Wier

Rascal: A Memoir of a Better Era by Sterling North

1963

WINNER:

A Wrinkle in Time by Madeleine L'Engle

HONOR BOOKS:

Men of Athens by Olivia Coolidge

Thistle and Thyme: Tales and Legends from Scotland by Sorche Nic Leodhas

1962

WINNER:

The Bronze Bow by Elizabeth George Speare

HONOR BOOKS:

Belling the Tiger by Mary Stolz

Frontier Living by Edwin Tunis

The Golden Goblet by Eloise Jarvis McGraw

1961

WINNER:

Island of the Blue Dolphins by Scott O'Dell

HONOR BOOKS:

America Moves Forward: A History for Peter by Gerald W. Johnson

The Cricket in Times Square by George Selden

Old Ramon by Jack Schaefer

1960

WINNER:

Onion John by Joseph Krumgold

HONOR BOOKS:

America Is Born: A History for Peter by Gerald W. Johnson

The Gammage Cup by Carol Kendall

My Side of the Mountain by Jean Craighead George

1959

WINNER:

The Witch of Blackbird Pond by Elizabeth George Speare

HONOR BOOKS:

Along Came a Dog by Meindert DeJong

Chucaro: Wild Pony of the Pampa by Francis Kalnay

The Family Under the Bridge by Natalie Savage Carlson

The Perilous Road by William O. Steele

1958

WINNER:

Rifles for Watie by Harold Keith

HONOR BOOKS:

Gone-Away Lake
by Elizabeth Enright

The Great Wheel
by Robert Lawson

The Horsecatcher by Mari Sandoz

Tom Paine, Freedom's Apostle
by Leo Gurko

1957

WINNER:

Miracles on Maple Hill
by Virginia Sorenson

HONOR BOOKS:

Black Fox of Lorne
by Marguerite de Angeli

The Corn Grows Ripe
by Dorothy Rhoads

The House of Sixty Fathers
by Meindert DeJong

Mr. Justice Holmes
by Clara Ingram Judson

Old Yeller by Fred Gipson

1956

WINNER:

Carry On, Mr. Bowditch
by Jean Lee Latham

HONOR BOOKS:

The Golden Name Day
by Jennie Lindquist

Men, Microscopes, and Living Things
by Katherine Shippen

The Secret River
by Marjorie Kinnan Rawlings

1955

WINNER:

The Wheel on the School
by Meindert DeJong

HONOR BOOKS:

Banner in the Sky
by James Ullman

Courage of Sarah Noble
by Alice Dalgliesh

1954

WINNER:

. . . And Now Miguel
by Joseph Krumgold

HONOR BOOKS:

All Alone by Claire Huchet Bishop

Hurry Home, Candy
by Meindert DeJong

Magic Maize by Mary and Conrad Buff

Shadrach by Meindert DeJong

Theodore Roosevelt, Fighting Patriot
by Clara Ingram Judson

1953

WINNER:

Secret of the Andes by Ann Nolan Clark

HONOR BOOKS:

The Bears on Hemlock Mountain
by Alice Dalgliesh

Birthdays of Freedom, Vol. 1
by Genevieve Foster

Charlotte's Web by E.B. White

Moccasin Trail by Eloise McGraw

Red Sails to Capri by Ann Weil

1952

WINNER:

Ginger Pye by Eleanor Estes

HONOR BOOKS:

Americans Before Columbus
by Elizabeth Baity

The Apple and the Arrow
by Mary and Conrad Buff

The Defender by Nicholas Kalashnikoff

The Light at Tern Rock by Julia Sauer

Minn of the Mississippi
by Holling C. Holling

1951

WINNER:

Amos Fortune, Free Man
by Elizabeth Yates

HONOR BOOKS:

Abraham Lincoln, Friend of the People
by Clara Ingram Judson

Better Known as Johnny Appleseed
by Mabel Leigh Hunt

Gandhi, Fighter without a Sword
by Jeanette Eaton

The Story of Appleby Capple
by Anne Parrish

1950

WINNER:

The Door in the Wall
by Marguerite de Angeli

HONOR BOOKS:

The Blue Cat of Castle Town
by Catherine Coblentz

George Washington
by Genevieve Foster

Kildee House
by Rutherford Montgomery

Song of the Pines: A Story of Norwegian Lumbering in Wisconsin
by Walter and Marion Havighurst

Tree of Freedom by Rebecca Caudill

1949

WINNER:

King of the Wind by Marguerite Henry

HONOR BOOKS:

Daughter of the Mountain
by Louise Rankin

My Father's Dragon
by Ruth S. Gannett

Seabird by Holling C. Holling

Story of the Negro by Arna Bontemps

1948

WINNER:

The Twenty-One Balloons
by William Pène du Bois

HONOR BOOKS:

The Cow-Tail Switch, and Other West African Stories
by Harold Courlander

Li Lun, Lad of Courage
by Carolyn Treffinger

Misty of Chincoteague
by Marguerite Henry

Pancakes-Paris by Claire Huchet Bishop

The Quaint and Curious Quest of Johnny Longfoot
by Catherine Besterman

1947

WINNER:

Miss Hickory by Carolyn Sherwin Bailey

HONOR BOOKS:

The Avion My Uncle Flew
by Cyrus Fisher

Big Tree by Mary and Conrad Buff

The Heavenly Tenants
by William Maxwell

The Hidden Treasure of Glaston
by Eleanor Jewett

Wonderful Year by Nancy Barnes

1946

WINNER:

Strawberry Girl by Lois Lenski

HONOR BOOKS:

Bhimsa, the Dancing Bear
by Christine Weston

Justin Morgan Had a Horse
by Marguerite Henry

The Moved-Outers
by Florence Crannell Means

New Found World by Katherine Shippen

1945

WINNER:

Rabbit Hill by Robert Lawson

HONOR BOOKS:

Abraham Lincoln's World
by Genevieve Foster

The Hundred Dresses by Eleanor Estes

Lone Journey: The Life of Roger Williams
by Jeanette Eaton

The Silver Pencil by Alice Dalgliesh

1944

WINNER:

Johnny Tremain by Esther Forbes

HONOR BOOKS:

Fog Magic by Julia Sauer

Mountain Born by Elizabeth Yates

Rufus M. by Eleanor Estes

These Happy Golden Years by Laura Ingalls Wilder

1943

WINNER:

Adam of the Road by Elizabeth Janet Gray

HONOR BOOKS:

Have You Seen Tom Thumb? by Mabel Leigh Hunt

The Middle Moffat by Eleanor Estes

1942

WINNER:

The Matchlock Gun by Walter D. Edmonds

HONOR BOOKS:

Down Ryton Water by Eva Roe Gaggin

George Washington's World by Genevieve Foster

Indian Captive: The Story of Mary Jemison by Lois Lenski

Little Town on the Prairie by Laura Ingalls Wilder

1941

WINNER:

Call It Courage by Armstrong Sperry

HONOR BOOKS:

Blue Willow by Doris Gates

The Long Winter by Laura Ingalls Wilder

Nansen by Anna Gertrude Hall

Young Mac of Fort Vancouver by Mary Jane Carr

1940

WINNER:

Daniel Boone by James Daugherty

HONOR BOOKS:

Boy with a Pack by Stephen W. Meader

By the Shores of Silver Lake by Laura Ingalls Wilder

Runner of the Mountain Tops: The Life of Louis Agassiz by Mabel Robinson

The Singing Tree by Kate Seredy

1939

WINNER:

Thimble Summer by Elizabeth Enright

HONOR BOOKS:

Hello the Boat! by Phyllis Crawford

Leader by Destiny: George Washington, Man and Patriot by Jeanette Eaton

Mr. Popper's Penguins by Richard and Florence Atwater

Nino by Valenti Angelo

Penn by Elizabeth Janet Gray

1938

WINNER:

The White Stag by Kate Seredy

HONOR BOOKS:

Bright Island by Mabel Robinson

On the Banks of Plum Creek by Laura Ingalls Wilder

Pecos Bill by James Cloyd Bowman

1937

WINNER:

Roller Skates by Ruth Sawyer

HONOR BOOKS:

Audubon by Constance Rourke

The Codfish Musket by Agnes Hewes

The Golden Basket by Ludwig Bemelmans

Phoebe Fairchild: Her Book by Lois Lenski

Whistler's Van by Idwal Jones

Winterbound by Margery Bianco

1936

WINNER:

Caddie Woodlawn by Carol Ryrie Brink

HONOR BOOKS:

All Sail Set: A Romance of the Flying Cloud by Armstrong Sperry

The Good Master by Kate Seredy

Honk, the Moose by Phil Stong

Young Walter Scott by Elizabeth Janet Gray

1935

WINNER:

Dobry by Monica Shannon

HONOR BOOKS:

Davy Crockett by Constance Rourke

Days on Skates: The Story of a Dutch Picnic by Hilda Von Stockum

Pageant of Chinese History by Elizabeth Seeger

1934

WINNER:

Invincible Louisa: The Story of the Author of Little Women by Cornelia Meigs

HONOR BOOKS:

ABC Bunny by Wanda Gág

Apprentice of Florence by Ann Kyle

Big Tree of Bunlahy: Stories of My Own Countryside by Padraic Colum

The Forgotten Daughter by Caroline Snedeker

Glory of the Seas by Agnes Hewes

New Land by Sarah Schmidt

Swords of Steel by Elsie Singmaster

Winged Girl of Knossos by Erik Berry

1933

WINNER:

Young Fu of the Upper Yangtze by Elizabeth Lewis

HONOR BOOKS:

Children of the Soil: A Story of Scandinavia by Nora Burglon

The Railroad to Freedom: A Story of the Civil War by Hildegarde Swift

Swift Rivers by Cornelia Meigs

1932

WINNER:

Waterless Mountain by Laura Adams Armer

HONOR BOOKS:

Boy of the South Seas by Eunice Tietjens

Calico Bush by Rachel Field

The Fairy Circus by Dorothy P. Lathrop

Jane's Island by Marjorie Allee

Out of the Flame by Eloise Lownsbery

Truce of the Wolf and Other Tales of Old Italy by Mary Gould Davis

1931

WINNER:

The Cat Who Went to Heaven by Elizabeth Coatsworth

HONOR BOOKS:

The Dark Star of Itza: The Story of a Pagan Princess by Alida Malkus

Floating Island by Anne Parrish

Garram the Hunter: A Boy of the Hill Tribes by Herbert Best

Meggy Macintosh by Elizabeth Janet Gray

Mountains Are Free by Julia Davis Adams

Ood-Le-Uk the Wanderer by Alice Lide and Margaret Johansen

Queer Person by Ralph Hubbard

Spice and the Devil's Cake by Agnes Hewes

1930

WINNER:

Hitty, Her First Hundred Years by Rachel Field

HONOR BOOKS:

A Daughter of the Seine: The Life of Madam Roland by Jeanette Eaton

Jumping-Off Place by Marian Hurd McNeely

Little Blacknose by Hildegarde Swift

Pran of Albania by Elizabeth Miller

The Tangle-Coated Horse and Other Tales by Ella Young

Vaino by Julia Davis Adams

1929

WINNER:

The Trumpeter of Krakow by Eric P. Kelly

HONOR BOOKS:

The Boy Who Was by Grace Hallock

Clearing Weather by Cornelia Meigs

Millions of Cats by Wanda Gág

Pigtail of Ah Lee Ben Loo by John Bennett

Runaway Papoose by Grace Moon

Tod of the Fens by Elinor Whitney

1928

WINNER:

Gay Neck, the Story of a Pigeon by Dhan Gopal Mukerji

HONOR BOOKS:

Downright Dencey by Caroline Snedeker

The Wonder Smith and His Son by Ella Young

1927

WINNER:

Smoky, the Cowhorse by Will James

1926

WINNER:

Shen of the Sea by Arthur Bowie Chrisman

HONOR BOOK:

The Voyagers: Being Legends and Romances of Atlantic Discovery by Padraic Colum

1925

WINNER:

Tales from Silver Lands by Charles Finger

HONOR BOOKS:

The Dream Coach by Anne Parrish

Nicholas: A Manhattan Christmas Story by Annie Carroll Moore

1924

WINNER:

The Dark Frigate by Charles Boardman Hawes

1923

WINNER:

The Voyages of Doctor Doolittle by Hugh Lofting

1922

WINNER:

The Story of Mankind by Hendrik Willem van Loon

HONOR BOOKS:

Cedric the Forester by Bernard Marshall

The Golden Fleece and the Heroes Who Lived Before Achilles by Padraic Colum

The Great Quest by Charles Boardman Hawes

The Old Tobacco Shop: A True Account of What Befell a Little Boy in Search of Adventure by William Bowen

The Windy Hill by Cornelia Meigs